OHIO
DOMINICAN
UNIVERSITY™

SINCE 1911

BY **JAMES MOLONEY**

HARPERCOLLINSPUBLISHERS

Black Taxi

Copyright © 2003 by James Moloney

Printed in the United States of America. For information address
HarperCollins Children's Books, a division of HarperCollins
Publishers, 1350 Avenue of the Americas, New York, NY 10019.
www.harperchildrens.com

Library of Congress Cataloging-in-Publication Data
Moloney, James, date.
    Black taxi / James Moloney.— 1st U.S. ed.
        p.   cm.
    Summary: When Rosie agrees to take care of her grandfather's
Mercedes while he is in jail, she gets more than she bargained for,
including being thrust into the middle of a jewel heist mystery and
being attracted to a dangerous boy.
    ISBN 0-06-055937-3—ISBN 0-06-055938-1 (lib. bdg.)
    [1. Crime—Fiction. 2. Mercedes automobile—Fiction.
3. Grandfathers—Fiction. 4. Australia—Fiction. 5. Mystery and
detective stories.] I. Title.
PZ7.M7353B1 2005   2003027848
[Fic]—dc22   CIP
                                                      AC

Typography by Andrea Vandergrift
1 2 3 4 5 6 7 8 9 10
❖

Originally published in 2003 by Angus & Robertson,
An Imprint of HarperCollins*Publishers*, 25 Ryde Road,
Pymble, Sydney, NSW 2073 Australia
First U.S. edition, HarperCollins Publishers, Inc., 2005

For my daughter Siobhan

ONE

Paddy Larkin is just a little bent. I don't mean he's one of those wrinklies you see walking along the street all doubled over like an upside down L. I mean he doesn't always stick to the straight and narrow. To put it bluntly, Patrick Larkin is a crook.

But he's a nice crook, and he wouldn't hurt a mouse. Steal the cheese from under its nose, yes, but hurt someone . . . not Paddy.

He also happens to be my grandfather. He used to tease me mercilessly when I was growing up, but in ways that let me laugh along with him. Once, when I was fourteen and starting to bulge in new directions, he said, "Rosie, you've got more curves than a racetrack. Those young boys will be lining up to hold your hand soon."

I hoped they would do more than hold my hand, but I didn't tell him that.

He was smiling when he said it and he gave me a hug, a real grandfather's hug that showed he loved me.

"Any boy who breaks your heart better watch out," he added solemnly. That didn't stop them, but it was great to have a grandfather who was looking out for me.

Paddy has been more like a father than a grandfather. As for my real father, hell, I haven't seen him for . . . To tell you the truth, I don't remember, and I certainly don't care. All he ever gave me was a surname. Sinclair.

It was Grandad who taught me how to drive, in his own car too, the Mercedes he loves so much, the one he bought from the funeral home when it went bust. (How a funeral home could go bankrupt when there's always people dying is something I never quite worked out.)

Actually, the way he snaffled that car says a lot about Paddy Larkin. He went to the auction of all the funeral gear just to see what was there, along with everyone else in Prestwidge—a sort of outing for the curious. There was the Mercedes-Benz, a 280S, one of those classic styles from the 1960s, and as soon as he saw it, he fell in love. "It's my one chance to have something special," he told Grandma. Perfect condition too. After all, no one's in a hurry to arrive at the cemetery, are they, so the engine was as good as new.

There were a few others taking a close look at the Merc that day so Grandad dropped a word here and there about why that funeral home had gone out of business. "Disrespect for the dead," he whispered with a knowing smile and tap on his nose, as though he knew all about it. "When the hearse was too busy to pick up a new corpse, they'd use this Mercedes, eh." He'd seen it with someone's feet sticking out the window, he told them.

There was also a pair of roof racks in the auction. Grandad spread the word that they were kept in the trunk of the Mercedes, and that when there was no room in the backseat, they'd strap a body to the top of the car. "Like a surfboard," he said, showing them his arm held rigid from elbow to fingertip. "It helped if they were already stiff, of course."

When the bidding started, no one seemed very interested in that black Mercedes. The auctioneer couldn't figure it out. Then Grandad put up his hand and the car was his. "Just business," he told me afterward. Who am I to argue? I love driving it.

I had to drive it on a Monday morning recently, to an event as sad as any funeral. We were taking Grandad to court. Despite all his clever wiles, Paddy Larkin had been arrested again. The first time he went up before a judge, years ago, the magistrate had thrown the case out because the idiot cops made a mess of the evidence. Mind you, the cops, the judge, the lawyers, and especially our family knew Grandad was guilty.

Then he got caught fair and square with three cartons of thermal underwear in the trunk of the Mercedes and another two in the backseat. Thermal underwear! You can imagine how embarrassed I was about that. This time the judge said he'd suspend the sentence since it was his first conviction.

First conviction! Ha! First time they could prove it, that was all.

But now he'd been picked up again. Three arrests in a career lasting thirty years is pretty good, if you ask me, but unfortunately the judge didn't agree. So it looked like Grandad was going to jail. In fact, his lawyer was pretty sure he'd get six months. He could probably do with a rest, considering how much he does around here. In fact, if there was one reason why the whole thing was unfair to my poor Grandad, it was that he only got caught doing a good turn, in this case for Uncle Bruce. That's Uncle Bruce the slimeball. Oh, don't get me started.

Uncle Bruce was sitting beside me as I drove the Mercedes that Monday morning. Behind us in the backseat, I could see Grandad's big face in the mirror. It was leathery, with deep creases around the eyes and heavy eyebrows, thick and bushy. He was in the middle, with Grandma crying softly on one side of him and my mother having hysterics on the other.

We were "his girls" as he called us—wife, daughter, and granddaughter. It was Grandma I felt sorry for. She must have been dreading that this day would come for a long time. She was dressed all in black, like one of those little Greek grandmothers you see round the streets sometimes. Bit odd, with a name like Larkin.

Grandad saw my eyes in the little frame of the mirror and smiled. "Eyes on the road, Rosie," he said, without sounding like a nag.

Normally, he'd be driving himself, but just as we were leaving, he tossed me the keys. "I can't drive and take care of these two at the same time," he whispered in my ear. So I was the chauffeur.

I'd only been asked along in the first place so there would be someone to drive the car back again afterward. Grandad himself would have to stay behind with the cops. (Oops, not thinking about that one.) And Uncle Bruce had lost his license for drunk driving. Second time, too. If he's caught again it will probably be him off to jail as well. Once he's driving again, I'm going to have a good sniff every time he comes round to borrow money from Mum, and if there's booze on his breath, I'll phone the police and turn him in. That sounds cruel, but if you're waiting for me to take it back you'd better find a comfortable place to sit.

That left the women to do the driving. Grandma was prone to fainting spells, including the one she had while she was behind the wheel of this precious Mercedes. Luckily, neither Grandma nor the car was damaged. As for Mum, well, it's usually her passengers who faint.

Cynthia Sinclair is the only person in the history of Prestwidge who had two accidents in the same driving test. Both happened while she was trying to parallel park. She managed to go all the way back into the car behind her, and then come forward into the car in front. "Just making the space big enough, eh," the policeman told his mates back at the station, laughing his head off.

She passed a year later at the fourth attempt, and ever since then, the people of Prestwidge have kept off the roads on Thursday nights about seven o'clock when Mum goes to do the weekly shopping.

My mother's hairdressing salon is called Hair by Sinclair, which I have always thought says a lot about her taste and imagination. Luckily, we aren't the least bit alike. My hair is black. Hers is orange. I *have* never and *will* never wear a leopard-skin print. Mum has a leopard-skin skirt, and worse, matching shoes. The skirt is too short and the heels too high. Really, old women should know when to give up. She is forty-three years old, for God's sake!

Grandad loves her, but I know he shares my opinion about her driving ability, so if there is one certainty in this life, it's that she is never going to drive his car. So I was called in, even though I'd had to take the day off from school. Real troubleshooter, that's me.

Actually, I should have already finished school by now . . . long story. The shortened version is that I left after sophomore year to be Mum's apprentice at Hair by Sinclair. Twelve months of watching my mother wear leopard skin was enough to make my Prestwidge High School uniform look like a Gianni Versace. So I went back to do my junior and senior years, and now I've got just one semester to go.

But on to the courtroom. We'd just crossed the bridge and were waiting in the rush hour traffic when the matter came up. "Who's going to have this car while you're inside?" asked Uncle Bruce.

See how his mind works. He didn't give a damn about his own father. He was already looking for the main chance, and this after Grandad had been caught with suspicious goods that really belonged to Bruce!

"The car," whispered Grandad. I guess when you're heading for jail, some details can slip your mind. He was worried about Grandma, of course. The fainting fits meant she couldn't live on her own, so just the day before we had agreed that she would come and live with us. But the car?

"I don't know," he mumbled. "It will have to stay shut up in the garage at home, I suppose."

Uncle Bruce saw his chance. "It'll need a run every now and then so the battery doesn't go flat. Tell you what, I'll pop round every week and rev it up for you." I swear his voice sounded like he was doing Grandad a favor.

"But you've lost your license."

"Don't need a license just to start it up in the garage."

"How are you going to get to our place when you can't drive?"

Bruce looked thoughtful, as though he were genuinely hunting around for a solution, when in fact he had it all worked out. "I know. The Merc can stay in *my* garage."

"There'll be plenty of room," I said maliciously. Bruce was forced to sell his rusty, bone-rattling bomb to pay for the drunk-driving fine.

Grandad wasn't falling for it anyway. "You'd drive it all over the place. Use it like it was your own, and before you know it, they'd nab you for driving without a license."

"I won't get caught. You don't have to carry round a flashing sign that says disqualified driver."

"How would you pay the fine? They'd impound the car and sell it out from under me," growled Grandad.

"I'm telling you, I won't get caught."

"No!" said Grandad firmly.

The car went quiet for a minute or two. Then my mother piped up. "Jason needs a car."

Grandad looked at her; Grandma stopped crying and looked at her. Uncle Bruce turned right round in the front seat to glare at her. I tell you, if I hadn't been watching the road, I'd have turned round to look at her too.

"What's the matter with you lot?" said Mum when she found all those eyes boring into her. "At least Jason's got a license."

Grandad snorted, as he does now and again when he's thoroughly disgusted. "He's got an empty head, that's what he's got. I don't like to speak ill of my own grandson, Cynthia, but he needs a good kick up the arse." Grandma nudged him in the ribs. "Sorry. Didn't mean to swear."

"If he had a car for a while, he might make something of himself," said Mum.

Ha! To make something of himself, my brother, Jason, would have to stand upright and walk around like a human being. I've seen slugs with more get up and go. He lives at home with Mum and me. Actually, he lives on the sofa in the living room, just like one of the cushions. Half the time, he doesn't even bother going to bed. I throw a blanket over him sometimes, and if Mum didn't bring him food, he'd be a skeleton by now.

The others were still staring at Mum in heated disbelief. "He just needs a chance," she said lamely. I doubt she believed it herself.

"NO," said Grandad again, even more firmly.

"Well, I guess it's up to me then," said Mum. "I'll come over once a week and take it round the block."

A look of absolute horror passed over my grandfather's face. "No, Cynthia. It will be all right." He had to think quickly. He saw me. "Rosie. Rosie can do it." Phew! He'd saved the day. I saw him smile broadly in the rearview mirror and grinned back at him. I love my Grandad.

I was heading into the parking lot under the court building now. I don't know what was happening in Grandad's stomach, but mine was tying itself into every knot in the Boy Scout handbook.

Just as I pulled up next to a brand new Mercedes that didn't look half as stylish as ours, Grandad looked at Bruce again. His eyes narrowed in suspicion, then he said, "Rosie, maybe you can do more than just take my car for a spin round the block. You're a sensible girl and a bloody good driver. How long have you had your license now?"

"Nearly a year, Grandad."

"No accidents?"

"Not one." (Well . . . but this was hardly the time to mention the little scratch I'd added to Mum's car. With so many already, she hadn't noticed it herself.)

"That's it, then. You're the one to take care of this car while I'm away. In fact, keep it at your place. Drive it around a bit with your friends."

And that was it. How to get a Mercedes without lifting a finger.

If I'd known then what I know now, I'd have said no, with a Paddy Larkin firmness.

TWO

Things didn't go so well in the courtroom that day. In fact, they went as badly as the lawyer expected. The case was really divided into what the police could prove (which looked bad for Grandad) and what they didn't even know (which was good for Uncle Bruce).

I knew the full story, and I constantly had to stop myself from jumping up in my place and shouting the truth to the judge and the prosecutor and the jury. If there was the least chance of getting Grandad off, I would have done it too. *Bruce is the one you want,* I would have told them. *Paddy doesn't do it anymore. For God's sake, Paddy Larkin is* RETIRED.

Mind you, it had been quite a career. He didn't steal the stuff himself very often. His usual game was to take a batch of stolen goods—clothing, or electrical things like videos—from the real thief, and shift them quietly around to people who ran a flea market stall or a secondhand shop. He thought of himself as more of a distributor. He had his own circle of customers, who trusted him because he was careful. Paddy Larkin was the one who could get you things on the cheap, particularly if you were hard up. A real humanitarian, a caring bloke, that's my Grandad and I mean it. It's called "redistribution of wealth." We learned about it at school.

(Of course, if you own a department store or a warehouse, you might not see it that way.)

But now he's retired. It was Bruce who forced him back into it, just for one last go. Bruce had "acquired" a load of clothing, but no one would buy it from him. He couldn't shift it, and it looked a bit incriminating sitting in his living room if the police ever called, which they did occasionally because they knew he was a slimeball as much as I did.

Grandad told him to dump it, but he wouldn't. He'd borrowed money from a loan shark to get hold of the stuff in the first place, and he had to make good on the deal. So against his better judgment, Paddy agreed to help.

He went round to GG's—that's the nickname for his mate George Goggin, who had a van big enough to hold all the junk in Bruce's living room. Together, Paddy and Bruce made the rounds of his usual customers. They unloaded all of it except for three parkas that Paddy kept back for some old people he knew who were having a hard time. He dropped off Uncle Bruce at the pub, but on his way to deliver the van back to GG's, the police pulled him over.

Dumb bad luck, it was. They were stopping every car in the area looking for someone else, but of course when they found Paddy Larkin in a van, they did a search.

What did they find? Three parkas, all the same, all brand new, and none of them Paddy's size. Even then, he might have talked his way out of it if Constable Enright hadn't been there. Who do you think had done the police report on the stolen clothing? In fact, he had been typing up the list of stolen goods in his own plodding, two-fingered style only an hour beforehand. He recognized the parkas, one thing led to another, and that's why we all ended up in a courtroom with Grandma crying quietly and my mother going off like a fire engine.

The jury did its job. Guilty.

Grandad stood before the judge. Six months, as expected.

We were given a few moments to say good-bye. Grandad went through his pockets. The wallet went to Grandma. When he saw me jingling the car keys miserably, he patted his coat and found one last thing. "Here, if you're minding the car, Rosie, you'd better take this." He handed me his cell phone. It was a little Nokia, brand new. Just as well the police didn't ask where he'd got it from. "Look, a few people might call you, to run an errand or two."

I gave him a worried look.

"Nothing illegal. I promise. Just driving people around."

That was what he said. Honestly. Just driving people around.

Ha!

Problem. How to keep Grandad's car away from Uncle Bruce. I did have to go to school the next day, after all. If I miss more than a day at a time, they tend to notice. Mum is at her salon all day, ensuring every woman in Prestwidge has the same hair style, a quest to which she has devoted her entire life.

Bruce lives a ten-minute drive away. With no car and no license, he couldn't drive, but if he had a friend, that wouldn't be a problem. Luckily, he hasn't got any friends. He hasn't got a wife these days either since the poor thing finally came to her senses last year and walked out, taking most of the furniture with her. Just backed a truck up to the front door, paid two apes to cart the stuff out for her, and that was that. (The story goes, she left the dog's basket in the middle of the bedroom with a note suggesting he sleep in it.)

But Bruce is a resourceful slimeball. He'll get here one way or another, and if I leave the Mercedes in our garage, I may as well leave the keys in the ignition. Hot-wiring a car is within his small repertoire of practical skills.

There was only one solution. I would have to drive the Mercedes to school and leave it in the teachers' parking lot. There have been so many thefts from the teachers' parking lot in recent years that they now lock the gates between nine and three.

The next morning, I was on my way to school when the phone rang. I'd forgotten all about it. Popped it in the glove box when we left the courthouse, and it was still there, still turned on. The glove box was too far for me to reach while I was driving. Let it keep ringing, I decided.

The noise stopped, then seconds later started up again, muffled by all the other junk I'd seen in there. Could it be for me? Sounds a bit ridiculous to think so, but there's something about a ringing phone. It's a girl thing, maybe. I pulled over and reached into the glove box. "Hello."

"Who's this?"

"It's Rosie Sinclair."

"Where's Paddy?"

"In jail."

"Shit!"

The phone went dead. I guess he didn't want to talk. That's a boy thing.

On to the teachers' parking lot. There's only one other student with a car at Prestwidge High School. Garret Hemmings has rich parents, and you'd expect him to be at a private school in the city somewhere. Well, he had been. He tried out three of them and got himself expelled from each one. Around Prestwidge, he's no more of a bad boy than half a dozen others I could name. I think that came as a shock to Garret, and nowadays he contents himself with the occasional outburst of colorful language at selected teachers. So what else is new? If that could get you expelled from Prestwidge, half the classrooms would be empty.

As I locked the Mercedes, I looked up. Josh Willmot was staring at me from fifty feet away. He took off quickly, and by the time I reached the schoolyard, the entire school knew.

"Where did you get it?"

"Who does it belong to?"

"Is it yours?"

"What kind of car is it?"

This last question was greeted with a rolling of eyes and a collective sigh of "Derrrr."

"It's my grandad's. He's letting me drive it for a while."

Just then, the A-list turned up. Justine, Clare, and Fiona. Justine was six feet tall and already acted like the model she wanted to be. "Wow, a car," she gushed, "and not just any car. A Mercedes."

"It's pretty old," someone pointed out, but the A-list ignored this. I was suddenly in the loop. With so much happening so quickly, I hadn't counted on the attention Grandad's car would bring me—and I certainly hadn't anticipated a blossoming friendship with the likes of these three.

My celebrity continued. By lunchtime, Justine and

company had decided that I could have the privilege of driving them around after school. "How about a ride?"

I know, I know. The answer should have been a Paddy Larkin "No."

But what the heck. It was fun having the bold and the beautiful hanging about, wanting something from me. I was Paddy's granddaughter and I knew how the world worked. If I did something for these three, with their manicured nails, their perfect hair, and their uniforms tweaked to look like a fashion statement, then I could ask for something in return. What exactly, I didn't have a clue, but that was half the fun.

After school, they were waiting for me, all three piling into the backseat. Where was my chauffeur's cap! I expected them to start waving like princesses off to the ball, but all their fancy airs and pretense shot straight out the window when they spotted a figure in the street.

"Oh my God, it's Todd Rooney."

It's impossible to describe adequately the pandemonium that accompanied this announcement. Squeals, shoving one another in the shoulder, jostling for the best vantage point when they were so tightly packed into the backseat. As for the dialogue that followed . . . No, I can't repeat it. Such turkey gobble is an insult to female intelligence.

All I glimpsed was a private-school blazer hanging from a frame tall enough to look Justine in the eye when she was in her highest heels.

"He didn't see us," Fiona wailed. "Quick, Rosie. Go round the block."

Yes, ma'am. Who was I to spoil the fun?

The traffic was heavy, which made the girls more agitated. "Is he going to ask you out, Jus?" Clare demanded.

"*I* don't know," she answered hotly. "I've only spoken to him twice."

"He's *so* hot!"

"What a hunk!"

"He's *gorgeous*!"

At least they were speaking in sentences again. The next step was to try for more than three words before the exclamation mark.

By now I had circumnavigated the mall. Target dead ahead. The relief that he hadn't disappeared into dust rang out loud and clear from the backseat. "Slow down, Rosie. Make sure he sees us this time."

I'd do more than that, I decided. The poor guy. His bag tugged savagely at his shoulder. How far did he have to go? I pulled up and, through the open passenger-side window, called, "Hi. Can we give you a lift?"

The backseat went strangely silent. A young man's face dipped low enough to peer in the window. Hey, it wasn't a bad face either. Olive skin, smooth, without a single acne scar, hair in place, even after a day at school. Todd Rooney smiled uncertainly at me, then looked in the backseat. "Oh, hi, Justine."

Someone behind me was laying an egg.

"We're not going anyplace in particular. Can we drop you somewhere?" I asked.

"Yeah, okay." He opened the door and pushed his heavy bag onto the front seat, sliding himself in beside it. Close up, he was even cuter, I must say. This wasn't such a bad idea after all.

Fiona retrieved her voice from wherever it had fled to. "Great car, eh!"

"A classic," Todd commented knowledgeably. He turned and smiled at her. Even with my eyes on the road, I could feel the heat of her blushing face.

"How's Mark?" Todd asked Justine, and from the conversation that followed, I gathered this was the connection. Justine's brother played football with Todd, and this was how they'd met.

Todd asked me to drop him home, just a few streets away, and gave me directions. Turning to speak to the girls in the backseat was a strain, so once we were away from the mall, he turned round and looked straight ahead through the windshield. When he wasn't looking at me, that is.

"Classic car," he said again.

"It's my grandfather's."

"Yeah, I've seen it around the place. Hard to miss a black Mercedes in Prestwidge." He kept talking as I kept driving.

This is not bad, I thought. If driving a black Mercedes leads to encounters like this, I'm going to enjoy the next few months.

"What's your name?" he asked as he was thanking me and getting out of the car.

"Rosie Sinclair."

"Rosie Sinclair," he repeated, as though this would help him remember it. I didn't mind if he remembered it at all. No, Todd Rooney, you say it over and over as many times as you like.

The A-list wouldn't speak to me—probably because Todd had shown more interest in me than in my passengers. My membership was to be short-lived, it seemed. What did I care?

After I had dropped all three girls off at Justine's house, the cell phone rang again. This time I pressed the answer button and just listened.

"Larkin?" said a voice after a moment or two.

It wasn't the same man as this morning. Of course it wouldn't be. That guy at least knew that Grandad wouldn't be answering his cell phone for a while.

"Larkin, is that you? Say something."

It's not like I was playing a game, teasing the man. The tone of his voice threw me off balance, that's all. I've never heard anything so threatening, and he had done no more than ask for Grandad. But whoever it was lost patience and cut the call.

Grandad's cell phone had all the bells and whistles, but as I punched my way through the menu options trying to read the number that had just called, it came up blank. Whoever he was, he didn't want to advertise his number over the airwaves. Hardly surprising in Grandad's line of work.

When I got home, I put the cell phone in my school bag for safekeeping. But the memory of that voice sent a shiver through my whole body, and for an instant, I felt anything but safe.

THREE

Prestwidge is what they used to call a "satellite town." I guess someone in an office building high above the city center thought it up decades ago as a way of keeping the riffraff out of their hair. So surveyors were sent out into the countryside and measured up streets and stuff so they could build little sweatboxes using cinder blocks and a complete lack of imagination, and then they dumped people in them who couldn't afford to live anywhere else.

Of course, over the years, the buffer zone of open ground between the city and these satellites like Prestwidge got filled up, so now we're just a huge suburb at the end of the railway line, a splodge on the map about one and a half miles across, marked "Battlers, No Hopers, and Petty Crooks."

If you were born in Prestwidge Hospital, they call you a Prestie. I was and so was Mum, so we belong here. It's not that bad, though to be honest, the high school's not the best. One year, every one of our seniors failed the final exams. The newspapers put their class photo on the front page, and there was such a fuss I thought the authorities would all come out and measure our heads or something.

What do they expect anyway? The place has bog-awful buildings straight off the Cheapest Possible page in the public works catalog. Some schools have lush turf on their playing fields; we've got crabgrass and dust. Some schools are freshly painted, and I suppose you could say ours is too, while the graffiti is still wet.

No one earns much social status by going to Prestwidge High School, so we Presties have to create our own status symbols. Just now, the absolute *numero uno* of status symbols is the cell phone.

The trick at first was to have it ring during class. Juvenile, I know, but it was a kind of victory over the demoralized teachers. Justine, Clare, and Fiona scored a huge coup the day they arranged for their boyfriends to ring at exactly the same moment. It was impossible to work out where the ringing was coming from, and the rings only lasted for three seconds. Just long enough for the rest of us to identify the signature tune of each. The teacher went ape. Not often I get a smile out of the A-list's antics.

This put them in second place in the all-time great "gotcha list," after the legendary Phil Greymouth. A teacher sent Phil next door to a rowdy classroom to find out why they were making so much noise. He stuck his head through the door and shouted at them in a voice that could be heard all over the school. "Shut up, will ya. We're trying to get some sleep in here."

Smart-arse comments can't be outlawed, but cell phones can. They must be turned off during class. School rule. Guess what happened on Wednesday. In the middle of math, Grandad's cell phone goes off like a burglar alarm. I scrambled pathetically to get at it, throwing everything out of my bag before Mr. Tudor's face went from purple to puce.

I stabbed at the buttons and turned the damned thing off. The kids all thought I was showing off my new toy, along with the Mercedes, and no amount of grovelling to Mr. Tudor would change their minds, or his. He raged at me for thirty seconds. A summary of what he said amounted to Don't Let It Happen Again, OR ELSE!

What should I do? Maybe it had been an important message for Paddy. At morning tea, I turned the phone on again. It began to ring sixty seconds later.

"Hello," I said tentatively.

"Ah, at last. Why did you cut me off before, Paddy. And for the last hour you've had your phone off the hook or whatever it is they do with those new things." The voice was accusing and mildly annoyed, but it wasn't the man who had sent chills up my spine. This was a woman, an old woman by the sound of it, though she'd found a bit of juice to tell Paddy off with.

"I'm sorry," I said politely. "Paddy's not here."

The woman hesitated. "What did you say, Paddy?"

"No, he's not here. This is his granddaughter speaking."

"Where is he?" she asked indignantly.

I didn't want to say precisely. "Er, he's . . . unavailable."

The old girl didn't think much of the excuse. "What do you mean, unavailable? He was supposed to pick me up half an hour ago."

"I'm sorry, but Paddy won't be picking anyone up for quite a while. He's . . . um . . . he's gone away. On holiday."

"He didn't tell *me*. How will I see my sister?"

"Get a bus," I whispered, though not loud enough for the bossy old dear to hear me. I looked at my watch. Three minutes until the bell. "Look, I have to go. Paddy will be back in six months or so. You can call him then. 'Bye."

There was something like a squawk down the line and some words as I hit the End button. I could make out a couple of them: ". . . dead by then . . . ," which put me a little on edge. Who would be dead by then?

Before I could turn the phone off, it rang again.

"Hello, hello. Young girl. Are you there? Speak up."

Young girl! Well, I suppose when you're eighty-something, then anyone under fifty is a baby. What could I do? "Yes, I'm here," I said.

"Who are you?"

"Rosie Sinclair. Paddy is my grandfather."

"Is he really going to be away for six months?"

"I'm afraid so. I'm sort of minding his stuff for him. His phone and his car."

"His car! You've got his car?"

"Yes, but—"

"Oh, that's a relief. Now, I really must get up to visit my sister. Can you come now? I'm already rather late."

Just then the bell sounded. Kids were moving to class and I was talking to an old lady who expected me to drive her to her sister's place, *now*!

"I'm sorry," I said firmly. "I'm tied up just at present."

"Well, what time can I expect you?"

Mr. Hoskins, the assistant principal, appeared in the yard. If he saw me with my ear to a cell phone, he would give me a detention for sure. I moved into the hall leading to my next class. "I can't come at all."

"Of course you can, dear. You've got Paddy's Mercedes, haven't you?"

"Yes, but—"

She cut me off again. "Will it be this morning?"

Mr. Tudor saw me from inside his classroom. I had to end this call NOW.

I've never been good under pressure. "I can't get away until after three," I said.

"Good. I'll expect you after three, then."

That was that. I was inside the classroom before I

realized that I didn't have a clue who I'd been talking to, let alone where she lived. In a way, this was a sort of revenge against the old darling who had left me so flustered.

At lunchtime, the phone rang again. "You don't know who I am or where I live."

"Sorry," I said meekly.

"Mrs. Foat." She gave me the address. "After three, then. I've let them know I'm coming."

Grandad had asked me to do a few errands, so I suppose it was only fair, like payment for having the car. After school, I refused all pleas for a lift and headed off to the address Mrs. Foat had given me, using the street directory from the glove box.

She seemed a frail old thing, but I wasn't fooled. I'd seen her at work, or heard her from the wrong end, anyway. Of course, now she was as gracious as the queen of England. "So good of you," she purred when I helped her down the steps. I wondered how she got up and down this staircase by herself.

The sister's name was Meredith and she wasn't in a house of her own, like Mrs. Foat. She was in the hospital. Poor dear. Her wasted body was still there in the bed, but her mind had left the building. Paddy Larkin wouldn't be out in time for this funeral. I could tell that much.

Mrs. Foat told me she would be ready to go home at five. That meant I was free until then, I suppose. Thanks a lot. I'll go have a smoke and polish the limo, I almost said sarcastically. Maybe I *would* need a chauffeur's cap after all.

Then it was back to Mrs. Foat's house. There didn't seem to be a Mr. Foat anymore, though there was evidence that a man had lived there once: the handyman repair to the back door that wasn't quite right and the dusty tools on a workbench in a room that ran off the kitchen. The photos gave the game away. She saw me looking at them. "He's been gone ten years. If it wasn't for those, I'm afraid I would have forgotten his face." She said all of this in a matter-of-fact tone, without a glance in my direction. She was a shrewd old thing, as I had learned, and she guessed what I was thinking. "That sounds terrible to you, I suppose."

Well, it did, to tell you the truth, but of course I didn't say so to her. What's love if you can't remember your husband's face? But she had moved on without looking at me.

"Here," she said, holding out her hand.

I opened my palm and into it dropped two dollars. "What's this for?"

"The ride, of course. I always pay Paddy."

Two bucks. Great! No wonder he turned to crime. But I thanked her, didn't I, and went home to find out which diet fad Mum was into this week. Just my luck.

Eggplant and lemon juice or something like that. I hate eggplant. Why doesn't someone come up with the hamburger-and-chocolate diet? Honestly, people have no imagination.

FOUR

t recess on Thursday, I sat with the phone in my hands. To switch on or not to switch on. That was the question. If this sounds like a familiar line, it's because we'd been doing *Hamlet* all morning.

> *Whether 'tis nobler in the mind to suffer*
> *The demanding phone calls of outrageous old folk,*
> *Or to turn my back on their sea of troubles,*
> *And by ignoring them, get a life.*

Sorry, Mr. Shakespeare.

I already had one gig for the afternoon. A Mr. Duval rang before I left for school. Paddy took Mr. and Mrs. Duval down to the shops each week. Late afternoon was fine. Not, *Please could they get a ride in the black taxi?* Just, *When!*

I told him four o'clock.

Why should I spend all afternoon running errands for my grandfather's friends? I had assignments and stuff.

Oh, all right. I had assignments, but I was more likely to spend my time doing stuff.

I do have friends, though to be honest, they mostly have jobs that don't finish until 5:00 P.M. and my best bud, Glenda, goes to the university and often has late lectures. But hey, I've got the keys to a fantastic car. I could just go cruising. Maybe see that friend of the A-list girls on his way home from the station again. All sorts of possibilities. Bugger them. I'm not a granny nanny.

Then, I had a flash of yesterday with Mrs. Foat. There was no bus route near her place. She couldn't go to see her sister unless someone took her. The stairs in and out of her house were dangerous. And two dollars! A cab would cost fifteen, in each direction. Thirty dollars was probably more than she spent on food for a week. What if she starved, just so she could afford to go visit her sister? She'd end up next to her in the cemetery before Paddy ever saw her again.

Bloody conscience.

The Duvals were charming in the old-fashioned way. They offered me a cup of tea before we started and asked about Paddy in a sensitive tone that told me, without actually using the word, that they had found out he was in prison.

"Isn't she a pretty girl, Eric," exclaimed Mrs. Duval, who told me to call her Janice.

"Pretty? Why, she's beautiful," he answered, topping her.

Mrs. Duval knew she had been trumped. She simply smiled and won me over with a chocolate biscuit. They made sure the last two chocolate biscuits were eaten on the day they went shopping for more. It was Mrs. Duval's biscuit that I was offered. The pair of them were quietly competing for my favor. What a wonderful old couple, I thought to myself, which I suppose sounds condescending.

During the drive to the supermarket we explored my place in the Larkin family tree. They knew more about my family than I did. I was so taken with their sweet and gentle ways that I joined them inside to push the shopping cart around. Maybe I was being manipulated by their charm, but they had it all over Mrs. Foat in that department.

Then, who did I spot but Todd Rooney. He had already seen me. Waved. He was coming my way. We all exchanged hellos, but he seemed uncomfortable. He thinks these two are my grandparents, I realized. "Just doing an errand," I said, worried how this would sound to the Duvals, but they had moved on.

"Me too. Getting a few things for Mum," Todd said, holding up a basket with the leafy end of some celery poking over the end. A lot of guys would worry they looked unmanly carrying a basket like that, but he didn't seem to mind, and he certainly didn't look unmanly from where I was standing. I wondered what the skin of his chin would feel like if I ran my finger lightly along . . .

Oh sorry. Just daydreaming. I still had the cart and the Duvals were waiting patiently for me at the end of the aisle. "Do you need a lift home?" I asked Todd.

"Wouldn't mind."

Neither would I.

Todd had everything he needed already, so he sauntered along beside me as I followed the Duvals. Don't ask me what we talked about. It was one of those nothing conversations where the fact that you were walking side by side was more important than anything we said.

"Don't forget the cinnamon, Janice," said Mr. Duval. "You know you don't enjoy your bingo without a bit of cinnamon cake."

How cute can you get? Grandad was partial to a bit of cinnamon cake as well, I remembered. Must be an oldies thing.

We took the elevator down to the parking lot where I had left the Mercedes, but as soon as I opened the door, I had the strangest feeling. I smelled smoke; not the smoke of an engine fire or burning upholstery, thank God, but cigarette smoke. Since I was trying to quit, and on Grandad's orders I hadn't let anyone else smoke in the car, this set the alarm ringing in my head.

The Duvals didn't notice anything and neither did Todd. There was no reason why they should. But that whiff of stale smoke made me suspect someone had been in the car. I looked around, but there wasn't anything in the car to steal except maybe the street directory in the glove box. Who would bother? If someone wanted to break in, surely it would be to steal the car itself. And how would they do it without leaving a trace?

You're imagining things, I told myself. Maybe the tobacco smell is on Todd's breath and you just haven't noticed it before. Everything seemed in its place in the glove box, as far as I could tell.

"What's wrong?" Todd asked me when he found me leaning awkwardly across him to explore it.

I settled back into the driver's seat. "Oh, nothing," I assured him, and by the time we'd left the parking lot, I'd put that unsettled feeling out of my mind.

With the Duvals in the backseat, there wasn't much chance to talk to Todd. He seemed intimidated by their presence and kept looking back over his shoulder.

When I pulled up outside his house, Todd asked me where I lived.

"Oh, way the other side of the school. Not far in the car though."

"No, I mean what street?"

I told him and he seemed relieved. The smile he gave as he said thanks hit me like a camera flash. Oh boy!

The Duvals saw it too. They'd watched and listened

every inch of the way. "What a handsome boy," Mrs. Duval said as soon as I'd pulled away from the curb. "And nice too. A real charmer."

There was no missing what she was getting at, but it was Mr. Duval who stunned me. "You know why he wanted to know what street you live on, don't you, Rosie?"

I acted dumb. Actually, I *was* dumb! Mr. Duval had to fill me in. "If you know a girl's name and where she lives, you can find her number in the phone book, can't you? Worked that one out for myself when I was a lot younger."

They had phones back in the time of the dinosaurs? I looked in the rearview mirror. The pair of them were smiling at me, that gentle friendly smile that had already won me over.

And I tell you what, Mr. Duval was right, because just after seven that night, Todd called.

"I hope you don't mind. I found your number in the phone book. Would you like to go to a party on Saturday night?" he asked.

I certainly *would* like to go to a party, particularly if it meant going with Todd Rooney! Justine, eat your heart out! The A-list would go ballistic if word got around that I was going out with Todd. Did I say "if"? It was more a matter of "when"—and if the rumors were slow in starting, I could always nudge them along myself.

Then at ten thirty, when I was thinking about bed, the cell phone rang. Maybe it was Todd. He can't do without me already. No, that sounds conceited. More likely to be some old codger wanting a lift. I hope I don't have to drive him to the hospital at this hour.

"Hello?"

"Where's Larkin? Tell him I want to speak to him." It was that awful, icehard voice from two days ago.

"Grandad's not here. You can't talk to him." Then like an idiot, I asked if I could take a message.

"Message!" says the voice. "Yeah, you tell him this. I want the ring."

"What ring?"

"He knows. Tell him I know he's got it and he'd better cough it up."

"I don't understand—" I started to say, but by then I was talking to myself.

FIVE

On Friday, the cell phone stayed silent right through morning recess and lunchtime as well. Maybe old people are too tired to go anywhere by the end of the week. When you're old, even doing nothing all week can get tiring. As for the guy who wanted that ring from Grandad . . . no news was good news.

I went to see Glenda after school. She's always home from the university by three on a Friday to get ready for her night job. (More of that in a minute.) Glenda is my closest friend, and because we talk every few days on the phone, she knew about the Mercedes. When I pulled up, she came out to kick the tires anyway. "Has he got a BMW he wants minded? Tell him I'm available."

Glenda had her education retarded by Prestwidge High School the same as me, but considering she was two years ahead (and two years older), it's a miracle that we ever got together at all. My mother's hairdressing salon was the connection. I wasn't enjoying school by the end of sophomore year, so when Mum suggested I pack it in and become her apprentice, I jumped at the chance. She's always considered too much education to be dangerous for a girl. "Like putting a V-8 engine in a cute little sports car," she said once. I think Mum's got a four-cylinder under the hood, if you get my meaning.

At the time I finished my sophomore year, Glenda had just finished her senior year. Because she desperately needed the money to get away from her booze-sozzled father, she started up as the other apprentice and promptly moved away from home. We hit it off straightaway, and just as well, too, because we both quickly discovered that we hated hair and heads and the smell of perming fluid.

The truth really hit home whenever we looked over at Tracey. She's been working with Mum for twenty years now. It's not that she's not a nice person or anything. She's quite good-looking for a fortysomething— wears tight little skirts that get the guys looking in the window, I've noticed. Despite having access to whatever hair color she likes, she's stayed a fine auburn for as long as I've known her.

She's very like Mum, which I suppose is why they get on so well together, and that was just it. Glenda and I looked at each other and realized that this was our life, as good as it was going to get if we worked out our apprenticeships. We didn't want to be just two more Traceys in a world already full of them.

But we were stuck for the whole of that long, long year—Glenda because she needed the money and me because my mother wouldn't let me mooch around doing nothing. (She already had a son doing that, after all.)

The thing about Glenda, though, is her ambition. She doesn't want to stay a Prestie all her life, and after a year working with the outside of people's heads, she announced that she wanted to work with the inside. She enrolled to study psychology at the university, starting the next year, and to everyone's surprise but her own, she was accepted.

The trouble was she wanted to go full-time, and that meant she couldn't hold down a day job. That's where this story gets a bit . . . well . . . exotic. Literally. To pay the fees, Glenda started up as an exotic dancer at a club in the city. Now, everybody knows that "exotic dancer" is code for something a bit more basic, so I should point out that Glenda has the sort of body that men undress with their eyes when she walks through the mall. All that's changed is that these days she gets paid to let them see what they spend so much time imagining. Makes sense to me. Some people would be disgusted, I suppose, but Glenda's motto is What you see is all you get. Her stage name is Giselle. Go, Giselle!

As for Rosie Sinclair, I found all this thoroughly inspiring (except for the stripping part) so I went back to finish my junior and senior years. There wasn't much else to do anyway and no one to do it with. The only Prestie girls who weren't in classrooms pushed a stroller in front of them wherever they went, and I wasn't going there, thanks very much. Anyway, school isn't so bad now. I won an academic award last semester. Third in math class. Mum liked the idea of my scoring good marks occasionally, but in math! I made a big show of shaving my legs just to reassure her.

"I've met a boy," I told Glenda, once she had stopped staring at the car. "His name's Todd. He's asked me to a party on Saturday night."

"Good-looking?"

"Gorgeous. And a bit shy too. He's so cute, I could wrap him up and take him home."

Glenda always cut straight to the important issues. "What will you wear?"

Oh God . . . and things had been going so well. I looked in the mirror. Long dark brown hair to my shoulders, little chocolate circles in the middle of my eyes, nice legs, a bustline that made boys look. I liked what I saw, even the little freckles on my nose. It was what I *couldn't* see that was the problem. I carry all my worries behind me—in my bottom, in other words. It's enormous. I could sell advertising space. There are islands in the Pacific Ocean smaller than my bum.

"Stop stressing about your bum," scolded Glenda.

"I can't help it."

"It's magnificent."

"Magnificently huge. That's the problem."

"Look, we've been over this a hundred times and I'm sick of it," she said with a genuine hint of warning in her voice. "You have the perfect backside. It's round; it's there. Enjoy it."

"Maybe I could get one side amputated and have the rest sort of spread out."

"It's not like peanut butter you can spread around on a piece of toast." Glenda gave me her exasperated look, so I backed off. Maybe I'd put her through all this just so she would say nice things about my bum. It can be a bit soul-destroying when you hang around with a perfect figure.

"The only butt you should worry about is this boy's," she reminded me.

"It looks pretty good to me. What I've seen of it through his school uniform, anyway."

She smiled. "It makes a change to be discussing *your* love life instead of *mine*."

That was the downside of being Giselle. Glenda had guys after her all the time, but they were all creeps. I kept hoping she would find someone nice. Maybe I had beaten her to it.

At least I could be sure she wouldn't steal him away from me, no matter how good-looking she was. That was the advantage of having a girlfriend two years older. All the guys my age were too immature for her. Mind you, I had my own problems in that regard. All the guys at school seemed so much younger than me. Little boys, really. All they talked about was football and beer and cars. Mum tells me that they never grow out of this, that even as grown men, their only topic of conversation will be football and beer and cars. She says I should count myself lucky they talk at all, instead of just grunting like baboons. I'm hoping she's got it wrong.

"How's it going with the geriatrics?" Glenda asked, to change the subject. I'd had to whine to her on the phone about my "errands" last night.

"None today."

I hadn't told her about the two calls from that cold and sinister voice or the smell of cigarette smoke in the Mercedes. I did now, as matter-of-factly as I could, because, to be honest, it all had me a little rattled. "How could a guy cram so much menace into a few simple words? And why would anyone break into the Merc?"

"Your grandad's car. That's serious," said Glenda with a worried edge to her voice.

"I'm not sure about the car. Could be my imagination."

"But not the phone calls," said Glenda as she fixed me with a concerned eye. "Do you know what ring he's talking about?"

"No. Grandad's not into jewelry. He doesn't even wear a wedding ring, and Grandma's fingers aren't exactly dripping with diamonds. Just her engagement ring. Nothing else. He reckons it's too hard to know what's real and what's fake."

"Well, someone thinks he's made an exception," Glenda commented. She picked up her bag. "Hey, can you drive me to the club? I can arrive in style for once. Should make the bouncers out front sit up and take notice."

So I did my chauffeur act again, willingly this time. It was worth it to see Glenda step out of the car. She didn't look like an exotic dancer slipping into a gaudy club that night. She looked more like a Hollywood star arriving at the Oscars.

Go, Giselle!

SIX

Saturday was the earliest we were allowed to visit Grandad in what they called the "correctional facility." Seriously creepy. High fences, razor wire, watchtowers. If Mum hadn't been crying already, this alone would be enough to set her off. And Grandma's a tough old bird in her own way, but I saw the blood drain out of her face as we drove into the parking lot. There wasn't much left in mine, I can tell you.

Paddy was as upbeat as he could manage, to save the feelings of "his girls," but I could see it was no picnic. You would think the Mercedes would be well down on the list of things to talk about, but there were lots of awkward silences that day, and one of us would jump in with a new direction for the conversation just to get the words moving.

"Have you had any calls, Rosie?" Grandad asked during one of those awkward lulls.

Any! Better to ask how many. I listed them off: Mrs.

Foat, the Duvals, and a few others I had managed to squeeze in between sleeping, eating, and going to school. He smiled widely. If this was what it took to raise his spirits, then maybe all those errands had been worth it.

"They just need a little help to get around, Rosie," he said. "Fiercely independent people, you understand. I appreciate it, and so do they, even if they'd never admit how much they need that car of mine. You made them pay, didn't you?"

"What! A dollar or two each. Yeah, I'll have enough to buy my own bar of chocolate soon."

Actually, that was just a slip of the tongue. It's not like I would ever buy a whole bar of chocolate just for myself (though if I did it would be the type with bright green mint inside). No, chocolate goes straight to my problem area, if you know what I mean.

Thinking about chocolate distracted me, but I could see what was going on. Grandad was manipulating me, of course. He knew I would do anything for him, and he had already guessed that I was a sucker for his bunch of equally manipulative eighty-year-olds. The more he beamed, the more I felt obliged to keep it up.

"Look, about the gas. I've got an account at Ferguson's garage on Pine Street. Fergo knows the car. He owes me a few favors. Just tell him who you are, and he'll fill it up for you as often as you need." He winked at me devilishly, and I couldn't help but wonder whether every oil filter and spark plug at that particular garage had made its way there legally.

Time was up. Hugs all around, a Niagara of tears, some of them mine.

I still hadn't been able to ask Grandad about the ring. How could I get a few seconds alone with him? To my surprise, he seemed as keen to have a private word as I was. Mum ushered Grandma off toward the door and here was the moment we needed.

"Rosie, Rosie," he whispered urgently. "Have you met the Duvals?"

I grinned. "Yes. They're so sweet. I took them shopping."

"Shopping. That's all, was it?"

The grin dropped from my face. He seemed rather agitated and eager to tell me something. "Look, I should have warned you about those two. It's the French blood, if you ask me."

French blood? What was he talking about? Mum turned at the door, looking as though she was about to charge back to Grandad and strangle him in another desperate bear hug. If I didn't ask my question now, I would miss the chance.

"Grandad, there was a call on your cell phone. The guy didn't give his name, but his voice was . . . well, it was sort of threatening. He said he wants the ring back."

"What ring?"

My heart sank. It wasn't just his words or even the tone of voice. The look on his face told me he didn't have a clue what I was talking about.

Then the guard was there, telling Grandad sternly that he had to go back through the heavily barred door. Paddy's last words showed that he'd forgotten about my question already. He was back to what seemed to matter most to him. "The Duvals, Rosie. Just be discreet. Okay?"

Discreet. He had me worried now. Were they into shoplifting? Should I search their cardigans before we went through the checkout?

I didn't have time to think any more about it. Mum and I had to get Grandma back to the car. She hadn't cried much but she seemed about to have one of her fainting fits all the same. Just as well I'd been getting lots of practice guiding old people around by the arm. Grandma wasn't so old really, but she sure seemed that way on our walk back to the Mercedes.

When we arrived back at our place, Uncle Bruce was there. Slimeball. I wondered how he'd made his way over here without a car or a friend to drive him. His wet clothes told the story. It had rained all morning and Bruce's jacket was just damp enough to show he'd been out in it for a few minutes here and there. Public transportation. How the mighty had fallen.

"Did you enjoy the bus ride?" I asked him maliciously.

He gave me a nasty look. It was all I could do to stifle a loud laugh. Absolute bitch, eh! I made a show of locking the Mercedes and slipped the key into my pocket.

"You should have come to the prison with us," chastised Grandma.

Ha! Bruce was afraid they would keep him there, where he belongs. I fantasized about him behind bars. Umm. Warm feeling. It's not like he cares about his own father in the slightest—I'm sure he only turned up at court to make sure Grandad didn't incriminate him.

"What are you doing here?" I asked him bluntly.

His narrow eyes opened wide. He'd been caught out. "Came to see you," he told Grandma. I guessed he was actually here to see Mum, and that normally meant he needed money.

Even Mum had worked this out, because she was glancing toward her handbag with a long face. Hair by Sinclair would never make us rich, but it paid the bills, due entirely to the fact that all the woman in Prestwidge *did* want to look the same and went to my mother to make sure of it. "How much do you need, Bruce?"

"Cynthia," he chided, his arms wide. "I haven't come looking for money."

Mum's face brightened for an instant; then the light went out. If he didn't want money, what *did* he want?

I made the tea and we sat around the kitchen table discussing Grandad. We were on to the second pot when I noticed that Bruce had gone missing. He obviously had a low sympathy threshold. I'd like to test his *pain* threshold, though.

If he wasn't in the kitchen, where had he gone? I

checked the living room, expecting to find him in front of the TV. Nope, Jason hadn't seen him, and there was no one in the bathroom either. He must be outside. My steps quickened then, because the only thing outside likely to interest Uncle Bruce was the Mercedes.

I was just in time. He had managed to break in without any trouble, and there he was, on his hands and knees inside the car, not the faintest trace of guilt on his face. "You're keeping it nice, Rosie," he commented. "Very clean."

"Grandad left it with *me*, remember. You haven't even got a license at the moment," I added cruelly.

He didn't seem hurt, and in fact he barely looked up at me. "Of course, of course," he muttered as he crawled along the seat toward the far door. "I wouldn't *think* of borrowing it without asking you." He had climbed out on the opposite side by this time and wandered back toward the house.

I locked the car and put the key in the pocket of my jeans as I followed. What could I have done if he'd gotten it started and driven off? I was hardly going to call the police when the first thing they would have done was impound the Mercedes.

But there was another matter that niggled at me as I returned to the house. He had been in the backseat, not the driver's seat. Since when did car thieves hot-wire the ignition from the backseat? There was something odd going on here.

SEVEN

Meet the Eisenberg sisters.

Appearance: pretty much identical. Tall and downright skinny, though to my eyes, anyone with a butt that doesn't hang over the edge of her seat is skinny. (Bloody problem area!) Both have shortish, schoolteacher hair, all of it gray.

Marital status: single. There was a suggestion that Caroline had a fiancé once, and of course there were the rumors about the Anglican priest, but neither has ever married.

Living arrangements: the Eisenberg sisters were born into a wealthy family in the leafy suburbs close to the city. However, the family fell on hard times, and these days the sisters live in a modest little house in Prestwidge. (Fell on hard times! That's about as far as anyone can fall and still remain on planet Earth.)

Age: no, they are not twins. Everyone thinks they are, because they look alike, but Deirdre is eighty-four and Caroline, a mere filly by comparison at eighty-two.

Favorite pastime: debating. (That's a euphemism. Go look it up!)

I knew all this about the Eisenberg sisters just from conversation around our house. Their mother was a world champion gossip, according to Cynthia, and it takes one to know one. They were members of every committee from the church auxiliary to the Returned Services League (war veterans) and then in retirement they founded the XYZ Club (Xtra Years of Zest—it's a thing for wrinklies to keep them chirping happily until they fall off the perch).

That was where they wanted me to take them when Caroline rang that Saturday—an XYZ function. I flicked the Merc into life and went to pick them up.

Now, I know my way around Prestwidge a bit, certainly round the mall and anywhere else where you are likely to find either a) decent clothes or b) decent guys. Other areas can be a mystery, I admit.

"Did Paddy tell you where to go, Rosie?" one of the sisters asked. I think it was Deirdre, though I was still learning which was which.

"No. I haven't spoken to Grandad much at all, really."

"We'll direct you then."

Famous last words.

The one I thought must be Deirdre jumped in first, since she had asked the question. "You get onto Maplethorpe

Road, as though you're going to Martindale—"

Caroline cut her off. "Heavens no. The poor girl doesn't want to be bothered with main roads at this time of day. Rosie, if you'll just take us to the end of the street and turn left."

I turned round in the seat and reached for the key in the ignition, but before I could start the engine, Deirdre made her counterattack. "No, not left. We'll get caught at the lights. They take forever to change at that intersection."

The contradictions continued. First I was to go one way, then the other would disagree. Anyone else I know who set to like this would have been shouting at each other by now, but not these two. Everything was said in the politest of gentle voices. But we were going nowhere. I couldn't make a start until they'd made up their minds.

Three minutes, four. Then it occurred to me. They weren't going to make up their minds. They were having too much fun, by the look of things.

"What's the actual address?" I asked from the front seat.

"Fifty-nine Timson Street," said Caroline.

"Fifty-three," said Deirdre.

It didn't matter. I had them now. In Paddy's street directory from the glove box, I looked up Timson Street. Easy-peasy. Once I had turned the first corner, the sisters stopped debating the best route and sat back to enjoy the ride. It wasn't very far in the end, and before I knew it, I was heading home again, my mind already grappling with the crucial question of what to wear on my date tonight with Todd.

Of course, this took up a lot of my concentration and didn't leave a lot for driving, but what happened next still wasn't my fault. It was the silver Commodore that cut sharply in front of *me*. I mean, you can't blame *me* for someone else's bad manners. No warning, no turn signal. It was almost like he was trying to force me into the gutter. Bloody lunatic. I wish I'd had time to catch his license number, because I would have put the cops on to him, even if I am Paddy Larkin's granddaughter.

It was more luck than good driving that avoided a collision. How could I have explained that to poor Grandad? And I bet the mongrel driving that silver Commodore wouldn't have stopped if he had put a dent in the Mercedes either, because he took off like a bat out of hell straight afterward.

The whole incident left me a little shaken, I must admit.

But the Mercedes didn't miss a beat, as though close shaves like that were just a part of life. Oh great! Now I'm taking life lessons from a car!

Glenda never gets out of bed before two on a Saturday, which is hardly surprising when you remember that

Giselle only finishes work at 5 A.M. After I dropped the Eisenberg sisters home again, I covered the backseat of the Mercedes with five different outfits I was trying to choose from for the big date and went round to see her.

"Skirt or pants, d'you reckon?"

"You've got great legs, Rosie. Show them off."

A skirt, then. But *which* skirt? Glenda didn't like any of the ones I'd brought with me.

"You want to knock his eyeballs out, don't you?"

She pulled out one of her own skirts (I've explained about Glenda's figure, haven't I?). I squeezed inside it, but only just. It was black, made of shiny fake leather, and very, very short.

"What does it look like from behind?"

"Will you stop obsessing about your bum!" She stood back for the view that I couldn't get of myself. "Fantastic," she said. "His brains will fry the minute he sees you."

She inspected the tops I'd brought with me. "This one." It was a simple pale pink affair and also rather tight in the best places. The view in the mirror wasn't half bad, especially my legs that I'm rather proud of. But that skirt . . . "I look a bit tarty, don't you think?"

"I'm not the one to ask. Come on. Be daring." It was her favorite line.

I caught a little of her resolve. "Okay," I said uncertainly.

My resolve lasted until I had to dress for the real thing. The pink top was cute but that skirt was too much for a first date. I put on my own little black skirt. *Much* better.

We had agreed that I would drive. Todd saw me pull up outside his house and came out onto the sidewalk to meet me. But instead of jumping in straightaway, he leaned through the window and invited me inside.

I sat there for a second with the cell phone in my hand before deciding to take it with me after all. If that scary voice called again, I had to know.

There was his mother, smiling warmly. She had the air of a nurse about her—a bad case of hat hair, flat shoes, and lips that didn't have to move to tell you what she thought of you. Thank God I'd switched outfits. Mr. Rooney came in from the kitchen and checked out my pink top (Hello! hello! My face is up here! That's better). I won a smile from him, too—a bit different from the one his wife had given me. Then it was good-bye to the parents and back to the car.

"Rosie, do you mind if we pick up some friends of mine along the way?" Todd asked suddenly, after we had driven three blocks.

Alarm bells went off inside my head. "Yeah, okay," I agreed reluctantly.

There were three friends, it seemed. Two guys from Todd's school and a girl named Alicia. The boys were weighed down by a six-pack in each hand. Alicia was weighted down by a ton of mascara. It set off her bleached blond hair nicely. If she was aiming for the tarty look, she had hit the bull's-eye.

The party was being held by one of Todd's private-school mates who lived well beyond Prestie territory. It was a twenty-minute drive and in that time Todd tried three or four times to get me talking. I kept my eyes firmly on the road and my mouth pretty well clamped. Inside my head though, the language was flying. *The rotten mongrel. He's just using me to get himself and his friends to a party. I'm nothing but a stupid taxi driver to him.*

When we arrived, he let the others go ahead, then looked me in the face. "Hey, listen. I'm sorry about that lot. They rang me at the last minute, desperate for a ride. But it's you I really want to be with." He took my hand and gave it a gentle squeeze and along with that lightbulb smile, it thawed me out a little. "Do you want a drink?"

"I'm driving."

He came back with a Coke for me and a beer for himself and told me how great I looked. The charm offensive was in full swing, and to be honest, it was working. He introduced me to a few people, and I could see the envy in the girls' eyes. Before long I was laughing along with the rest.

There was a live band out in the backyard and when they started up, Todd asked me to dance. Now, as it happens, I'd rather dance than eat chocolate (not that I *ever* do that!), so he didn't have to ask twice. The band was great but the real surprise was Todd. So many guys are self-conscious when they dance, making pathetic little movements with their hips and hands that show they just want the set to finish so they can get back to drinking. Not Todd Rooney. He was jumping like a demented Masai warrior—one with impeccable rhythm.

The real surprise came during the break. "Hey Rosie, come and meet the band," he said, dragging me along by the hand. They greeted him like a soul brother, and I soon discovered that they were all his classmates too, a garage band out on their first gig.

Next thing I know, Todd has the drumsticks in his hand and he's nestling in to drum the next set. He was fantastic. I danced in front of the bass drum, feeling the vibration hit me like a bomb and waving away any guys who wanted to dance with me. Try dancing with a whole drum kit sometime. It's awesome.

By the time the police arrived, I'd lost the feeling in my legs. Alicia, meanwhile, was off her face and Todd's two mates weren't much better. The cops didn't bust anyone, but they decided that since it was already after midnight everyone should go home. We managed to get all three of our passengers into the car, but Alicia really didn't look well. Every time she lay back in the seat she complained of feeling sick, but when she tried to sit upright, her head flopped around like a sleeping baby's. A half mile from her place, it finally didn't matter whether she was sitting up or lying back. "I'm going to be sick," she announced.

"Not in this car, you're not," I said rather heartlessly. I managed to pull over without causing a major accident. Just in time, too, because Alicia let rip like Vesuvius before we could even get her out of the car. The boys copped a good deal of it. "Oh shit. That's disgusting," one wailed. We could barely hear him above the moaning of dearest Alicia.

I opened the door, dreading the scene I'd find behind me, but Todd was out of his seat already, helping Alicia onto the grass by the sidewalk. He held her shoulders while she was spectacularly sick again, then cleaned her up and his mates too. They were lucky he was there. I'd been ready to drive off. We dumped them at home eventually, and thanks to Todd, their stink went with them. I drove to his place.

So.

There we were.

Parked.

Outside Todd's house.

All the lights were out except for one over the front porch. Nice touch. We did the small talk thing about what a great night it had been.

Things went quiet.

He thanked me for doing all the driving.

Things went quiet again.

Then he kissed me. Once. A sort of smooch that lasted about three seconds flat, and before I knew it he was on the sidewalk, smiling that electric smile. Like a robot, I started the engine and moved forward so he could wave me off to the end of the street.

And that was that!

EIGHT

"Now let me get this straight," said Glenda. "He kissed you good night but you can't make up your mind whether you're pleased or disappointed."

She was sitting on the kitchen bench, a bowl of cereal balanced in one hand, a spoon in the other, even though it was already three o'clock on Sunday afternoon. (Giselle worked Saturday nights as well.)

I nodded uncertainly in answer to her question.

"Okay, so let's review the facts." This was another of her favorite sayings. She put down the bowl and the spoon and started to count off the evidence with her fingers.

"Fact one: He's handsome."

I nodded.

"Fact two: He's fun to be with. Three: You had a great time. Four: He's a great dancer."

She had four fingers poking out from her palm now. I shrugged a shoulder and sniffed. "Yes, yes, and yes."

"He plays drums like a rock star." Glenda's thumb

shot out stiffly. A sigh from me.

She was becoming exasperated. "And . . . ," she said, forgetting her fingers in a heated effort to bring me to my senses. "And . . . as well as all that, he cares enough about his drunken mates to clean them up, get them home, and make sure there's no mess in your grandfather's car."

"I know. I know."

"No, you don't," she said indignantly. "You don't know how awful guys can be. Believe me, I do! Come down to the club sometime and I'll show you what they're like when they grow up a bit. Look, scientists should be cloning this bloke's DNA. Every girl on the planet should get one at least once in her life. Standard issue on your eighteenth birthday."

I sat there like an idiot. Maybe I *was* an idiot.

"Is he going to ask you out again?"

"He rang this morning to thank me for going out with him."

"HE RANG YOU THE NEXT MORNING!" (The capitals are because she was shouting.) "I've *got* to meet this guy." Glenda raised her eyes to the ceiling, then twiddled her fingers to show that she'd run out of places to count all Todd's good points. "Rosie Sinclair, your hormones need a good talking to."

I deserved that telling off. What more could a girl ask for? It had been a great night with Todd. I had really, really enjoyed myself. Who could dream of a better date? So what if, at the end of it all, he kisses me like I was his Auntie Rose from the nursing home? It was only a first date. If he'd been all over me, I would have had to fend him off and that would have been embarrassing, and he wouldn't have been able to ring me in the morning except to apologize, and then I would have had the upper hand in the relationship, and I didn't really want that anyway.

What am I saying? Just rambling, I suppose. I just wish he'd been a bit more . . . God, I don't know.

There hadn't been any more calls about the missing ring all weekend, and I had pretty well decided it was all a mistake. Maybe the guy with that creepy voice had found the stupid thing somewhere else. Not that he was likely to let me know so that I could stop worrying. Inconsiderate mongrel! By Monday afternoon, I was starting to forget all about it and just enjoy the Mercedes for the fun of it.

On the way home from school, I noticed it was low on gas. Grandad had said something about a gas station on Pine Street. It wasn't far, so I steered in that direction and soon found the sign, FERGUSON'S AUTO CENTER. It must be the last independent service station left on Earth, and to be honest, it looked as if a strong gust of wind could carry it off to heaven. Most people in Prestwidge buy their gas from the big glossy places with their flashy signs and gaudy colors. Ferguson's was a kind of oil-stain gray.

The thing about independent service stations is, well, the service. Not that I realized this. I had climbed out of the car, still in my school uniform, when a guy came to fill the tank for me. I didn't notice him until he called to me. "I'll do that for you," he said.

"No, it's okay. I can . . ." I looked up from the gas pump. Bang. It was like a karate kick in the chest, right through onto my heart. He was wearing jeans over leather ankle boots and a T-shirt that fitted tightly across his abs and around his biceps. His hair spilled out behind his ears, all bronze and golden curls, the tips brushing his shoulders, one of which was adorned with a fetching smear of grease where he had wiped his hand. His chin was strong, its lines faintly blurred by a day or two's growth, just enough to make it look intentional.

Oh boy! Smile, smile. Were the muscles of my face doing the right thing?

He seemed to be waiting for something. At last, he reached forward. "May I?" He took the nozzle from my hand. I think I said something intelligible. Maybe I just said, "Thanks."

He turned away to the car and slid the nozzle into place. This gave me a chance to look down at myself, to make sure everything was in place. Shit, my school uniform, an outfit deliberately designed by witches to make girls look ugly enough to crack mirrors. Why hadn't I gone home and changed?

My eyes hurried back to that body. I didn't think

guys wore jeans like that outside old cowboy movies. A flick of his head tossed the curls out of the way. I think my heart missed three beats. Did I sigh? I hoped not, but I must have made some sound because he turned his head toward me and smiled absently without parting his lips. It wasn't just that he was good-looking . . . I put my hand on the door of the Mercedes to steady myself.

"You can get back in your seat, if you like. I'll take care of everything."

"No. It's fine. I like standing."

Yes! I actually said that. *I like standing.* What a moron!

"Would you like me to look under your hood?" Oh, you bet, mister, but he meant the car of course. "Er, yeah, sure."

My eyes followed him to the front of the Mercedes. Again he hesitated, staring patiently at me. Blue eyes. Definitely blue.

"You have to pull the handle to release the hood," he said.

"Oh, right." Idiot. I did as he asked and moments later my view was blocked by the stupid hood. I moved to the side and watched as he checked the oil and the water and whatever.

"I've seen this car around the place. Old bloke was driving it."

"That's my grandad. He's letting me drive it while he's . . . out of town."

"Lucky you. Great piece of machinery. Classic lines." He stood back, admiring the Mercedes. I hoped he might notice some other classic lines and turned a little to give him my best angle. It was hopeless. Bloody school uniform. Even Glenda had looked like a nerd in this, so what chance did I have?

I took off into the office to see about paying—or not paying, if Grandad had told me the truth. The gorgeous guy strolled away like he owned the entire world and it was time for an inspection.

"Well, hello. It's Rosie, isn't it." I turned away from the window to find a much older man beaming at me. "You're Paddy's girl."

"Granddaughter," I said. This must be Fergo, I decided. "Grandad told me I could get his car filled up while he's . . ."

The smile disappeared from Fergo's face. "How's he doing in there?" he asked solemnly.

I gave him some equally solemn reassurance. It was like talking about a death in the family—which it was, I suppose, though at least Grandad would come back to life after six months.

"Look, er, there's no charge for the gas," Fergo told me.

"Are you sure? It seemed to take quite a lot."

"No worries. Your grandad used to take my mother over to the doctor every week before she passed away."

This didn't surprise me at all. I was staring out the

window again toward the black Mercedes. "Mr. Ferguson," I said, careful to sound casual. "Who's the guy . . ." Oh dear. What was his job? What did you call them? "The one who pumps the gas for you?"

Fergo looked out through the grimy window, but there was no one to be seen. "Could be any one of my fellas. What did he look like?"

I gave Fergo a verbal sketch but it left him puzzled. "Sounds like a male model the way you describe him. The only young bloke I've got here is my grandson, Darren, and he's ugly as a sack full of . . ." When he realized he was talking to a girl and not some grease-stained mechanic, he left the sentence unfinished. "Oh, now wait. I know who you mean. Yeah, my sister's grandson. He hangs round here a bit, working on his own car. He's got a good pair of hands actually."

I bet he does. I was wondering about that myself, though maybe not in quite the same way. "Does he have a name?"

Fergo straightened up and looked through the glass again as another car pulled up. "Chris," he answered, surprised that anyone should be so interested. "Chris Meagher."

NINE

There was a message from Glenda waiting for me at home. It said that she had something important to tell me that she didn't want to discuss over the phone. And I *definitely* had something to tell her.

As soon as I had changed out of my uniform, I headed over to her place, which she shares with two other girls. Neither of them was home when I arrived, so Glenda answered my knock.

"I've just seen the most *gorgeous* guy," I said breathlessly before I was even through the door.

Glenda rolled her eyes. "I know. You kissed him and turned him into a frog."

"No, not Todd. This is a new guy. His name's Chris Meagher."

Glenda was walking ahead of me down the hall toward her room, but when she heard the name, she stopped dead in her tracks. I was too excited to really notice. I swept straight past her, into her bedroom, prattling on about the gas station and his curls and those jeans. Then finally, I realized she didn't seem impressed.

"I know him," she said, and in a rather flat voice. "He was in my class at school for years."

"Was he as hot then as he is now?"

"He was hot," she said with more eye rolling.

Despite these words, Glenda had definitely gone cold on my story. I gave up. "What did you want to tell me about, anyway?" I asked her.

Her mood changed instantly. She closed the door of her room, even though her roommates weren't home, then sat on the end of her bed, which creaked on its springs. "You mentioned a ring the other day, right? Something to do with that man who called your grandfather's cell phone?"

It was a huge change of topic, but I managed to drag my thoughts away from tight T-shirts and curls long enough to nod.

Glenda lowered her voice even further. "I asked around the club on Saturday night, but no one had heard about a missing ring. Then this morning, before I went to class, one of the bouncers called me. He'd made a few inquiries on his own to try and impress me, and he heard about this robbery, going back weeks ago. A jewelry store on Gresham Street was knocked over."

Ring. Jewelry. It wasn't hard to see the connection. And Glenda had done more than just make the connection. She had dates and more details to pass on. "When was your grandfather arrested?" she asked.

I didn't exactly know the date by heart. "Hang on. It was the day I helped Mum out at the salon because Tracey had to get one of her ex-husbands out on bail." (That's Prestwidge for you. We all know where the police lockup is.)

When we checked a calendar, the dates matched. "It was the same night!" I said, becoming excited. "It *must* have something to do with this guy on the phone. He thinks Grandad is fencing the stolen jewelry!"

But before I could speculate any further, Glenda threw a wrench in the works. "They got all the stuff back, though. The diamonds or whatever, all of it."

"You mean they caught the thief?"

"Sort of. The cops are pretty sure it's a man named McWhirter. Trouble is, the poor guy's in the hospital, in a coma."

"A coma!"

"That's what the bouncer told me. He was hit by a drunk on a bicycle. This McWhirter whacked his head on the pavement when he fell." (Only in Prestwidge!)

"And he had the jewels on him."

"No, not a thing, but he's got a record long as your arm apparently, and the cops have him pinned as the prime suspect."

"So how did they get the diamonds back?"

"Found them. They were all in a plastic bag the cops discovered in a vacant lot near the jewelry store.

According to my bouncer friend, the thief botched the job and had the police coming from everywhere. He must have panicked when he heard the sirens and tossed the bag away in case the police nabbed him."

"But if all the stuff was recovered, why is that nasty voice calling Grandad's phone?"

Good question. No answers. After a pause, Glenda asked, "Do you think you should call the cops?"

"Who, me? Paddy Larkin's granddaughter? He'd drum me out of the family!"

"But they might know something we haven't found out yet."

She had a point, but it's never that easy for someone in my family. "I can't just waltz into the police station and start asking questions. What if Grandad *did* steal a ring somewhere along the line? He could end up in jail for six *years* instead of six months."

"We'll phone them, then. Anonymously."

"They can trace calls straightaway these days. Even pizza places can do it."

"We're talking about the cops here," Glenda pointed out. "They're not as smart as the guys at pizza places."

That was true, but I still thought we should be careful.

"We'll call from a pay phone, then." There was one on the corner, not far from Glenda's, and surprise, surprise, it hadn't been vandalized since the last time they fixed it. I rang the number and asked for the detective who was on the jewelry store case. A few clicks later, a heavy male voice said, "Yeah, Morgan."

What should I say? I hesitated. "Oh, um, I wanted to know about that jewelry store robbery a couple of weeks back."

"You want to know about it? What do you mean?"

This was terrible. The guy thought I was an idiot. "I'd like to know some details."

"Details! Listen, what's your name, for a start?"

My name. Oh God. "Er . . ." I looked around. "Giselle."

Glenda's eyes just about exploded from their sockets. "What are you doing?" she hissed. "There's cops in the club all the time, getting a free peek. He'll recognize my name!"

The policeman hadn't heard this. In fact, he didn't want to know much at all. "You expect me to believe your name's Giselle? Look little honey, you don't sound so old to me. If this is some kind of joke, I've got better things to do."

"No, no. I'm serious. I need to know about the stuff that was stolen in that robbery."

"That information is confidential. If you're doing a school project, you should find some topic that doesn't waste people's time."

"Was all the jewelry found? They say it was recovered on the night of the robbery."

"Well, whoever 'they' are was right. Now, if you'll excuse me . . ."

"No, wait. Is there a ring still missing?"

Now it was the detective's turn to hesitate. "Why did you ask that?"

"Well, was there?" I asked bluntly, feeling a little more confident now. His voice had changed, as though he wasn't quite so ready to get rid of me.

"Now listen, young lady. If you've found a ring somewhere, you should hand it in to the police."

I stayed quiet.

"You *have* found something, haven't you? Would you like to describe the ring to me?"

"So there *is* a ring still missing from that robbery?"

He thought about his answer for a moment. "Yes," he said finally. "Now, if you'll just describe the ring you've found, I can tell you if it's the one we're looking for."

"No, thanks," I said lightly, as though I had just ordered a Meat Lovers with extra pepperoni then changed my mind. "I've found out all I wanted to know."

I put the phone back on the hook.

"So, there *is* a missing ring," said Glenda, once I'd closed the door of the phone booth behind me.

I nodded slowly while I tried to work things out.

"Your grandad wasn't in on that robbery, was he?"

"Of course not."

"Well, whoever is making those calls on your cell phone thinks he was."

"No, he couldn't have had anything to do with it. He

was off shifting gear for Bruce that night. He'd borrowed a van and everything."

"Where was his car, then?"

"I don't know. Parked outside his mate's place until he came back with the van, I suppose."

"And where was that?"

I threw my hands in the air. "Glenda! How would I know?"

"Don't get snippy," she snapped. "What I'm saying is, maybe the Mercedes is part of this."

I was about to tell her she was crazy when the penny finally dropped. "The cigarette smoke," I whispered.

Glenda stared at me, waiting for an explanation. I didn't keep her waiting long, though she had to follow me on the run back to her house to hear it. "On Thursday, when I took the Duvals shopping, there was the smell of stale cigarette smoke in the car."

"What?"

"Don't you remember? I told you about it days ago. I took the Duvals shopping, and when we came back to the car, there was a smell of cigarette smoke inside."

"So someone must have broken into the Mercedes after all. Did they take anything?"

"Nothing to steal except the car itself, and there wasn't any sign that they'd tried it. They must have just been searching it."

"For that ring?"

"It looks like it now, doesn't it."

By this time, we were back at Glenda's place, where the Mercedes was parked in the driveway. She started on the passenger side; I searched the driver's side. Nothing under the seats or in the crevice between the cushions. Nothing hidden behind the dash.

"What about the trunk?"

"It would have been locked."

"Yeah, but if they could get into the car, they could get into the trunk, don't you reckon?"

I opened the trunk for the first time since Grandad had given me the keys. Nothing.

"They've been in here, though, searching," said Glenda. She leaned forward and pointed to a crease mark running diagonally across the carpet that lined the trunk. Tiny pieces of grit had collected in the crease when it was folded back, making the line easily visible. There was hard evidence, then, that I wasn't dreaming or making things up. This was as real as that sinister voice on Grandad's cell phone.

Glenda and I searched under the carpet and in the tool kit, then checked out the wheel jack, then went back to the interior to try again. It was at this point, with Glenda going through the glove box and me in the backseat, that it hit me. Uncle Bruce! Now I knew why I'd found him in the backseat of Grandad's car. He wasn't trying to steal it, I said to myself. He was searching it too.

I told Glenda how Bruce had come to visit us on

Saturday. "He knows something," Glenda said with a sly grin on her face.

"The bastard," I muttered. We went back inside Glenda's house, where I rang his number. No answer. Just his machine, asking me to leave a message. "You mongrel," I said, then put down the phone. He wouldn't be able to figure out it was me—and I'll bet I wasn't the first person to leave a message like that for Bruce Larkin.

TEN

With missing rings and old people using me like their own personal taxi driver, I wasn't paying much attention to school. I don't mean the classes and study and all that. I mean the built-in radar that alerts me to potential disaster and generally keeps my life out of the toilet was temporarily on the blink.

After break on Tuesday morning I left Grandad's cell phone on, didn't I. Next thing I know, it goes off like a fire alarm in the middle of Mr. Tudor's science class. He went ballistic. Can't say that I blame him really, with the rest of the class laughing and cheering like I'd just scored some big-time hit to make fun of him.

"Out," he shouted. "See Mr. Hoskins and maybe you'll explain to him why you feel free to disrupt my lesson."

How can teachers tell you off with such perfect grammar? I trudged down to the office and told the secretary I had to see Mr. Hoskins.

"Join the line," she said. Sarcastic smart-arse.

I sat down beside two unbearably smug freshmen. They reeked of stale cigarettes, which, in view of my recent experiences, didn't endear them to me much.

"What'd you do?" one of them asked.

"I stabbed two chicks for blowing smoke in my face," I answered. It took a moment or two before they worked out I just *might* be exaggerating.

The door opened and the nicotine-stained pair sauntered off to their fate. But that visit to the office wasn't all bad. There, on the chipped and unsteady coffee table in front of me, lay a mess of yearbooks. If Chris Meagher had been in Glenda's class then . . . I found the right year and flicked through impatiently until I found him. He looked so young and of course his hair was shorter, but all this made him even cuter. Under the portrait, his name was spelled out. Not Chris or Christopher. His real name was Christian Meagher. I loved it.

I searched for him among the sports teams. Football, basketball. He looked even better in a jersey and shorts, with those muscles on show this time. There were informal photos scattered through the pages as well, snapshots taken at dances and on school trips. There he was, at the center of a group gathered round a picnic table. He was giving the camera a serious glare that demanded the world take him seriously. But this wasn't what I noticed first about that picture. No sir. Another face caught my eye. A very familiar face. There was Glenda beside him, and around her waist, holding her too tightly against him, was the arm of Christian Meagher.

The door to Mr. Hoskins's office opened again. Out came the two girls, though this time there was no swagger in their step. Both faces had gone white and one of was sniffling pathetically into the back of her hand. My mouth went dry. It was my turn.

That bloody phone. All it did was land me into trouble. I thought about leaving it switched off—permanently. Or letting the battery run down maybe. No one could reach me then. I'd be free as a bird. But even as I thought about it, I knew I couldn't let those dear old things fend for themselves. How would Mrs. Foat see her dying sister? How would the Duvals get down to the shops? I had to admit as well, that in the back of my mind, I was still worried about that sinister voice. What if he hadn't found the missing ring? He might think I had it. If he couldn't get me on the cell phone, he might decide to visit me in person. I certainly didn't want that.

I went to see the crew from the A-list, who were speaking to me again. They were more likely to know about cell phones than anyone. Justine filled me in, and at lunchtime, I set up my voice mail.

Later, on the way home from school, I looked at the gas gauge. Damn. The little needle was still touching F. Not that I cared about gas consumption or anything. It was the guy who sold the gas that I was thinking about. I drove the long way home. Didn't do much good. Still full. Luckily, I was due to take Mrs. Foat up to the hospital. After I had driven her home again, I called the Duvals to see how their supplies were going.

"We're a bit low on sugar," Janice told me, "but don't worry. We can stretch it out until next week without any bother." So I took them some sugar.

After a few more completely unnecessary kindnesses like this, by the next afternoon the needle in the gas gauge had finally fallen a little below the F. Time to ponder a new fashion dilemma. What does a girl wear when buying gas? I pulled every item out of my wardrobe, one after another, and held each one up against me in front of the mirror.

No way.

Fashion disaster.

Old maid.

So yesterday.

At last everything I owned lay discarded on my bed. Who was I kidding, anyway? I already knew what I was going to wear. I put on Glenda's skirt and tried to see myself from behind. Nearly put my neck out. Oh, bugger it. I'll just make sure Chris looks at me from the front. I ironed the same pink top I'd worn to the party on Saturday—it had just been through the wash. As for makeup . . . well, I thought I was being rather restrained really, until Jason spotted me from the sofa, where he was hibernating for the decade.

"Jesus, look at your face! Did you just win a whole lot of free samples or something?"

That should have been a warning, but did I take the hint? Not Rosie Sinclair.

At Ferguson's garage, I parked the Merc beside the gas pump and got out eagerly. A gust of wind reminded me how short Glenda's skirt was. Then a figure appeared from the workshop . . . but it wasn't the one I expected. Yuck, pizza features. This must be Darren and he was every bit as repulsive as Fergo said he was.

"Fillerup?" I nodded and he went to work.

"Where's your friend?" I asked.

"Friend?"

"He was here on Monday."

He thought about this for a minute. "Chris, yeah, he's here. Hey, Chris!" he shouted. A few seconds later, there he was, striding toward me, in a different T-shirt this time but the same body underneath. "Hello, again," he said. "Rosie, is that right?"

How does he know my name? I wondered. I smiled. I think maybe "I beamed" would be more accurate. He looked at me, that hair dancing lightly around his forehead in the breeze. I wanted to brush it aside for him and see his whole face unobstructed, but before this pleasant little fantasy had gone far, the pump clicked off. Darren adjusted the nozzle, but after another second or two, the flow stopped again.

"It's full," said Darren. He looked at the numbers on the panel. "Seven dollars, sixty. Hardly seems worth you coming in."

"Oh, I was just passing and I thought I might as well have a full tank."

They glanced at each other and then laughed—at me! In fact, Chris now stood staring at me openly, admiring everything that he could see. This was what I had come for, it was why I had squeezed into a skirt one size too small and a hundred miles too short, but it was hardly how I had planned the meeting. That smirk on his face was becoming downright haughty. "You're Paddy Larkin's granddaughter, aren't you?"

I nodded, hoping this would get a bit of conversation going, but that full-of-himself smile was unsettling me more and more. Then it came to me. He knew my name and who I was because Fergo had told him—and that wasn't all Fergo had said. He must have been told how I'd asked about him on Monday. Oh God. I was making a total fool of myself. He knew I didn't need gas. He knew I had come just to see him, and there I was in Glenda's skirt and my face all made up. What was I *doing*?

I quickly pulled open the driver's door, but as I slipped in behind the wheel that damned skirt rode halfway up to my armpits. Through it all he stood there, watching and chuckling like he was God's gift to women and I had come along to beg for my tiny share of such a wonderful present.

I was furious—with myself, mostly. It was all I could do to keep the Mercedes going in a straight line. Once I regained a bit of composure, I realized my mind had already decided on the best course of action. Confession is usually the quickest way to feeling better. I would confess my stupidity to Glenda and let her tell me what an idiot I was. Then I'd get angry with her and forgive myself. It was the perfect system.

Glenda opened the door when she heard my knock, then looked me up and down. "Don't tell me, you've been to audition for my job at the club, right?"

"Shut up," I said, steaming past her and heading straight for her room.

"I'll get the chocolate," she called after me in a knowing tone.

That was another reason why the car had steered itself in this direction. Glenda always had a supply of mint chocolate in the fridge. Somehow, she managed to make a midsized bar last two weeks, nibbling a piece now and then and even forgetting about it for a week at a time. No stress in her life, that's why. She arrived with two rows—from a family-sized bar, my eagle eye noticed. She handed me one row and kept the other.

The chocolate was cold and hard and delicious. I let the warmth of my mouth thaw it out a little before sinking my teeth into the soft minty middle. Was there a more comforting sensation in the whole world?

"Okay, what did you do?"

I explained.

"You're an idiot," Glenda announced obligingly.

"But he's gorgeous. How else am I going to make him notice me?"

Glenda should also have obliged me with a deprecating laugh at this point, and that was how it all should have ended. There's nothing like a good laugh to remind us how unimportant boys are in the scheme of things. Instead, she frowned. "He's a bad one, Rosie. Forget it."

Well, if she wasn't going to play by the usual rules, I'd change them too. "I had a look through some old Prestwidge High yearbooks the other day. Chris's real name is Christian. Did you know that?"

Of course she knew that. She waited, knowing what was yet to come.

"You were in that yearbook too, Glenda. Sitting next to him."

"All right. I knew him."

"Knew him! An anaconda would have had a looser grip around your waist."

"So we had a thing for a while."

"What's 'a thing'?"

"That's personal."

"How long's 'a while'?"

"A few months. Look, Rosie, I'm serious. Chris Meagher is bad news. You don't want to get mixed up with him."

I waited, staring at her.

"That's it. I'm not telling you any more. We went out for a while. We broke up."

I pressed her, with pursed lips and raised eyebrows, just to see if what she really wanted was for me to make her spill the whole story. But her face hardened. This was one story I wasn't going to hear—not right now, anyway.

I went to the kitchen. In the kitchen was the fridge, and in the fridge was the chocolate. I broke off one more row, looked at the rest of the bar in my hand and thought, What the hell? and took the lot back to the bedroom.

The break had given me a chance to think, and I had to admit Glenda was right. Chris Meagher *was* bad news. I mean, how arrogant was he? And how *insulting* to stand there staring me up and down like that!

The trouble was, Glenda's warning hadn't put me off. If anything, I felt more intrigued—yes, even excited.

She watched me closely from across the room. She could read me like a book. "What about Todd?" she asked me. "The perfect date."

"*Almost* perfect," I responded sharply.

"Okay, so the guy needs a few kissing lessons. You could be his teacher."

I shrugged.

Glenda went on the attack. The hand was up again in front of her face. The fingers twiddled. "Remember, Rosie. He's got a lot of major pluses in the boyfriend department. You should give him a chance."

"It wasn't just the kiss. I tried to tell you. There just wasn't any spark."

"Yeah and Chris hangs around a gas station. One spark and you'll go up in a ball of flames." Her hands flew apart extravagantly.

I knew she was right. "It's my stupid hormones. They need a good talking to, like you said."

"Looks to me like you're a little keen to take them for a walk round the block. You know what I think? I think I'd better be your leash."

"No, it's okay. He's not likely to ask me out, now is he?"

"See! You're still thinking about it."

I was, too.

"Promise me, Rosie. Promise me now. If he ever asks you out, you'll say no."

I gave her an uncertain glare from beneath hooded eyelids.

"Promise," she demanded.

"All right, all right. I promise."

Glenda looked pleased at last.

I looked down at the silver wrapping. Oops. No chocolate left.

should have known what to expect when something so unusual, so completely unprecedented, occurred without any kind of warning.

On Thursday, at precisely 8:27 A.M., my brother Jason got off the couch. I thought at first he was proving a point to Grandma, who had been giving him merry hell about his laziness ever since she moved in with us. She had already cleaned the house from top to bottom, including a thorough vacuuming of the sofa while Jason was still lying on it.

More surprising still, he spoke to me in a sentence instead of an incomprehensible babble of grunts and gestures. "Rosie, could you do me a favor?" he entreated eloquently.

Of course, he wanted something from me, but hey, that's a form of communication too. "Careful there, Jason," I warned as he stood in front of me. "Make sure you're steady on those legs before you try walking. They might have atrophied."

He didn't have a clue what "atrophied" meant, but he knew from my tone that I was having a go at him. "Funny girl," he sneered. "A real comedian." Then he remembered he needed a favor and the sneering vanished. "It's my mate, Ben. He's moving. He needs a lift with all his gear."

"The Merc's not a moving van, Jason. Let him hire a truck."

"No, no. He hasn't got any furniture or anything. Just a few bags."

"You can't borrow the Mercedes."

"Yeah, I know you're touchy on the subject. Grandad gave it to you to mind, and you're gonna take good care of it. I'm cool with that. But maybe you could drive him. There's no buses where he's living now and taxis are like, *so* expensive." (Expect for Rosie's black taxi, that is).

Like a fool, I asked where he was living. It was out in the sticks a bit, but not so far. I could open up the throttle on the Merc for a change. Oh, what the heck. "Yeah, okay."

"Thanks, Rosie. You're a great sister." Yeah, a regular Girl Scout.

I wasn't going to miss any school to do this bloke a favor, not when I was already in trouble with Mr. Tudor.

"That's okay," said Jason. "When you get back would be cool." He stretched out on the couch again, so he could rest up for the big adventure.

It was already after four by the time we headed out of Prestwidge with the windows open and the radio turned up as far as it would go. I felt a little guilty that I hadn't tried to get hold of Uncle Bruce to see what he knew about the missing ring. There had been a couple of mysterious calls to my new voice mail—no words, just long silences and then a rude click, as though the caller was frustrated that I wasn't there to be yelled at. I guess I was still hoping the whole thing had blown over, so I just settled in for the ride.

Jason wasn't such bad company when he got off his butt. He dabbled a little with a band that let him sing, and he could keep a note pretty well when he put his mind to it. It was his couch potato body that let him down.

We were out among some small farms by the time he pointed out the turn. The farms were old, desperately poor and falling down, with rusting machinery dotting the paddocks, and only the occasional pathetic horse or goat watching us as we passed in a cloud of dust, with motor roaring. Then another turn, this time onto a rutted track, with evidence of civilization in sight.

"Not far now," Jason assured me when I complained about damage to the Merc.

He was true to his word, strangely. Another half mile

and we were swallowed up by thick forest. In among the trees, a house, or a hut really—no, not even that, more a shanty—appeared. Jason's friend Ben had heard us coming (little wonder) and was already outside waiting, with some bags at his feet. When I got out to meet him, I saw two of the bags were grubby tote bags, but the third was a black plastic garbage bag tied at the top with some adhesive tape. It bulged at the sides.

"What's in there?"

Ben looked down at the black bag, then at Jason, as though he was hoping my brother would answer for him. "Just clothes and stuff. I didn't have anything else to put 'em in."

Ben obviously came from the same school of hard work as my brother. I opened the trunk and he dumped the two tote bags carelessly inside. He was more cautious with the plastic bag. I would be too, I suppose. If it split, his few worldly possessions would be all over the place.

Then it was back to civilization—though that's stretching the word a bit when it was only Prestwidge we were heading for. I steered away from the mall and the business district, sticking to the suburban streets.

We were cruising easily along Hedges Avenue when I got the shock of my life. A police siren sounded briefly, right in my ear. In the rearview mirror, I could see the patrol car with its lights flashing. "Shit. They want me to pull over," I said to the others. "What have I done?"

What indeed! I was well under the speed limit, all the lights worked, I hadn't run a red light or a stop sign. I pulled over and scrambled out of the car, aware vaguely that Jason and his mate were doing the same. Behind us, a cop closed the door of his car and came slowly toward me. I recognized him from Grandad's trial. Name of Enright.

"What's wrong?" I asked, with an innocence and confusion that I didn't have to fake.

"Nothing, I hope, miss. It's just that I know this car pretty well, and I was surprised to see it on the road."

"Because the owner's in jail, you mean?"

He couldn't stop the corners of his mouth from curling up in satisfaction. "You're Paddy's granddaughter, aren't you? Well, I suppose that explains why you're driving it around. Nice car," he added, in genuine appreciation.

By now, I had relaxed. This wasn't so bad, then. The cops were just checking that no one had stolen Grandad's car while he was inside. Considerate of them, really. I tried to weigh up whether I could get away with a sarcastic remark along those lines. I glanced over at the other two to make sure they were creating the right impression. There was my brother staring anywhere but at the policeman, and looking decidedly uncomfortable. His mate Ben had disappeared.

"Where'd your friend go?" Enright asked Jason.

"Who?"

Oh, great. That was the best my stupid brother could come up with. He was going to deny there had been another bloke in the car. Enright might be a copper, but he wasn't entirely stupid. "Don't play games, son. There were two passengers when I pulled you over. Where's he gone?"

"Oh yeah. Him. Right," said Jason, as though he'd just remembered. I didn't know whether to groan or just cry. "Er, my mate, yeah, he was in a hurry. He's gone on ahead. On foot."

That helped me make up my mind. I groaned.

Constable Enright meanwhile looked down the road. No sign of the missing passenger, and of course now he was suspicious. He came closer and stared into the backseat, expecting to find someone crouched out of sight. This gave me a moment to slip round to where Jason was standing, or rather hopping from one leg to another, as though he were a three-year-old desperate to find a bathroom.

"Where's Ben?" I whispered.

"He took off."

"I know that, you idiot. What's going on?"

"He was afraid the copper would look in the trunk."

The trunk! It took me exactly one and a half seconds to make the connection. "That bag. What the hell's in it?"

Jason gave me a worried look. That was nothing compared to the look I gave him. "Tell me," I hissed menacingly.

"It's just some leaves."

"What kind of leaves?"

The frown became a pathetic wince. "Grass," he whispered.

"Grass clippings! What's he carrying grass clippings for?"

"No, not *that* kind of grass," he breathed in exasperation.

At last I understood. "Mari—" I managed to stop myself just in time, because I had sort of raised my voice a little, which was hardly surprising in the circumstances. I forced my voice into a whisper again and said, "You let your mate put a squillion bucks' worth of dope into Grandad's car, with me driving it?"

He offered a pathetic look as his reply.

"And now the bastard's taken off."

"Yeah, well. He can't afford to get caught, can he? Be third offense for him."

Constable Enright had satisfied himself that our friend wasn't hiding in the car. He called me around to his side. "What's your name?"

I told him politely, hoping he would just go away. Who was I kidding?

"Well, Rosie," he said. "I wasn't thinking of searching your car when I pulled you over, but since this mysterious third person has run off, it's all starting to look a bit suspicious. I'd like to look in the trunk if you don't mind."

Oh, great. And what will he find? Two tote bags with a bunch of unwashed rags belonging to Ben somebody and a black bag stuffed full of marijuana. They would have me in a cell next door to Grandad before I could blink!

I looked back at Jason. He was no help. He was standing there looking like a condemned prisoner at the foot of the gallows. Think quickly! Think quickly! Oh God, I wish I were good under pressure.

I looked up at Enright, who was being remarkably patient through all this. "Open the trunk, please," he said calmly.

I couldn't let it happen. Once that trunk was open, we were finished.

"This is police harassment," I said.

He look at me as though I'd farted. "What's that?"

"Harassment," I said again. Then I just let the words come, don't ask me where they came from. "I haven't done anything wrong," I said, louder this time, as I warmed up. "There I was, just driving these guys"— oops—"my brother around the place, well under the speed limit, and you pulled me over for nothing at all. It's not fair, you know. Just because my grandfather has a criminal record doesn't mean that the rest of the family is like that." Except for Uncle Bruce, of course. "I might be driving Grandad's car, but that doesn't mean I'm involved in a crime, does it?"

Constable Enright continued to look at me rather

strangely. His expression said, *Where is all this coming from*? Out loud, he said, "I just want to look in the trunk."

"The trunk. You want to look in the trunk. Well, where's your search warrant?" Search warrant! Hey, that was good. Must be all those TV shows. Yeah, I knew my rights. They had to have a search warrant to go hunting in the trunk of your car.

"I don't need a search warrant to look in your trunk."

"Oh, don't you?" I said, disappointed. So much for TV shows.

"No, not if I have reasonable cause, and since one of your passengers has run off suspiciously, I have all the cause I need to think maybe you're hiding something illegal."

"Now there you go again," I raged. "Illegal! What right have you got to accuse me of doing something illegal? I'm still at school, you know. Just a schoolgirl. What would an innocent schoolgirl be doing with something illegal in her trunk?"

"I don't know," said the policeman, exasperated. "Until I see in the trunk, I'm not going to know if you *are* carrying anything illegal in the first place."

"There you go again. It's all about poor Paddy Larkin, isn't it? Once the cops have got you, they never let go. They stick you in jail for hardly anything at all, and then they start harassing your family." I went on like this for a full minute, repeating everything I had said before. All the time, I was desperately hoping that something would fall from the heavens to save me, but it didn't. I was just putting off the inevitable and making Enright mighty mad at the same time.

"Just get out your keys and let me see inside the trunk," he demanded, losing patience rapidly.

By this time, I had worked myself into an absolute frenzy, more because of Jason than the poor copper. You can't open the trunk. That one truth kept hammering in my brain. The keys, you can't let him have the keys, or he'll open the trunk himself.

The keys were in my pocket. I pressed my palm gingerly against them and felt the edges. "The keys?" I shouted, hoping that this, too, would bring some solution. "You want the keys? Well, okay, if you want the keys, here they are!"

I pulled them out of my pocket and looked at them, glinting and heavy in my hand. "If you want them, then there, you go and get them!" And with a huge heave, I tossed them as hard as I could over Jason's head, toward the sidewalk. Maybe a serpent would rise up out of the ground and swallow them. Maybe an alien spaceship would swoop down from the sky and carry them off to Jupiter.

We stood there, all three of us, just watching the keys fly through the air. In my desperation, my fear, my anger, I had found more strength than I knew I had. They sailed high over my brother's head, then still higher, then finally began to arc downward. Just as I expected to see them fall with a clang on the sidewalk, they disappeared.

"Shit, Rosie! They've gone over the fence!" said Jason.

It was a high fence too, with wooden pickets looming at least six feet high, each sharpened to a point. Even so, the tops of overgrown trees sprouted thickly above them.

"This is ridiculous. What the hell have you got hidden in that trunk? The way you're going on, you'd think it was a dead body." Yeah, mine! "What could be so important?" demanded Enright.

"It's the principle," I announced self-righteously.

"Principle, my arse. You're hiding something. Now, you go and find those keys!" He was furious now.

I folded my arms. "You want them, *you* go get them."

"Get those keys, or I'll arrest you!" he threatened.

What the hell. If he found that bag of dope he would arrest me anyway. "Go right ahead. But you'll still be the one who has to find my keys." Did I really say that? It was all a bluff, of course. If he took a single step toward me I would probably start crying like a baby and beg him to let me go.

But it seemed I had made him think again. The good constable had no intention of scaling that fence and scrambling about in the undergrowth to find the keys. I can work up a fairly determined pout when I try, and he could tell I wasn't going to do it either. He glared at me. I glared at him. We were like two gunslingers in an old western on TV.

Then he saw Jason, idling about helplessly. "You!" he bellowed. "Find those keys."

"Me? I didn't throw them in there."

Police tempers are not renowned for being generous, and unlike me, Jason didn't have a pout that could frighten rhinos. His most determined look is more a plea for mercy. It didn't work on Enright. He took a few threatening steps toward my brother, and Jason suddenly changed his mind. "All right, all right."

He backed away toward the gate. It was an equally high affair, built of the same rough wooden pickets. Attached to this gate was a faded sign. ENTER AT OWN RISK.

"Hey, look at this. What's it mean, do you think?"

"They've probably got a rottweiler," said Constable Enright, smiling grimly, and he wasn't far wrong. Just then, a German shepherd came trotting over to see what all the noise was about.

"Well, that's that," said Jason with relief. "If I go in there, I'll be ripped to pieces."

"If you stay out here, you'll be ripped to pieces," was the policeman's reply.

I didn't hear the rest of this conversation. A utility truck had pulled up across the road. I turned to give the driver a *mind-your-own-business* glare, then gulped. It was Chris Meagher, and he was already out of the truck and heading across the road toward me.

TWELVE

"What's going on, Rosie?" Chris asked.

"I've lost my keys," I said.

"Where'd they go?"

I nodded toward the fence where the policeman and my brother were still arguing over how to get the keys from the German shepherd–infested yard.

Chris looked puzzled. "How can you lose your keys over a fence like that—and what's Enright doing here, anyway?"

It didn't escape my notice that he seemed to know the policeman. What's more, he had uttered the man's name without the least hint of affection. I would worry about that later, though.

For now, I was still embarrassed by my last meeting with Chris Meagher. At first, I had just wanted him to go away, but I was desperate, and after all, doesn't a drowning person cling to any buoy that comes along? (Sorry, that's an accidental pun, but come to think of it, this expressed my feelings at the time quite well.)

In as few words as possible, and with my voice low in case a certain word escaped too loudly, I explained.

He laughed. (Bastard.) Then he thought about it all, and that huge smile disappeared. "Actually, you're in deep shit."

"Thanks for saying that."

"What are you going to do?"

"I'm hoping to die in the next few minutes. Other than that, I don't have a plan."

On the sidewalk, the struggle continued, joined now by the incessant barking of the German shepherd. God, look at the size of it. I've seen race horses smaller than that dog.

"If he finds that dope in your trunk, you'll end up down at the lockup. You don't have another key on you, by any chance?"

"Of course not."

"Well then, we'll have to find another way."

I was about to ask him what the hell he was talking about when Enright called to me from the gate. "Get over here, young lady. Look at the bother you've caused."

He hadn't even noticed Chris. I looked over my shoulder as I took my time across the sidewalk, and all I could see was Chris heading back to his truck. Well, great. Seems we didn't create enough entertainment for Mr. Golden Curls.

The details of what followed are hazy in my mind. I

know that Jason did eventually go into the yard to get the keys. He wasn't mauled because Constable Enright is a bit of a dog lover, and he managed to calm the vicious beast down enough to slip one loop of his handcuffs round the collar and lock the dog to the gatepost. There was a lot of growling and shouting, and whether he did it on purpose or not I don't know, but he lost control of the German shepherd just long enough for Jason to get bitten on the butt as he was scuttling through the gate with the keys. He clutched at his jeans and hopped around howling as though the dog had ripped his entire leg off. What a baby. I couldn't see any blood. No blood, no sympathy, as far as I'm concerned, and the good constable was laughing so hard I thought he was having convulsions.

So the keys were back in our hands. Well, Constable Enright's hands, anyway. He snatched them from Jason as he was unsuccessfully avoiding those gnashing teeth. "Okay, let's see what you two are so keen to hide," he said triumphantly.

How long do you get for possession of marijuana? I was wondering. What would Mum say? What about Grandad? He was always telling us to stay away from anything illegal like that. But I was all out of ideas. There was nothing I could do now to stop Enright from opening the trunk. Once he knew what was in that black bag, my life was over. I'd end up with a police record. Everyone in Prestwidge would know about Rosie the

Dope Dealer. I started to shake, as though the temperature had suddenly dropped below zero. This was *serious*!

We followed him back to the car, and that was when I noticed Chris Meagher hadn't left after all.

"What are *you* doing here, Meagher?" Constable Enright growled. There was definitely a history between these two, then.

"I'm a friend of Rosie's," he answered confidently. "I was just passing and wondered what the trouble was."

"Well, stay back. This is none of your business."

Unfortunately, it was *my* business, though. I stood watching as the key was fitted into the lock and the lid of the trunk swung upward. We all stared inside, all except Chris, who had backed off a few feet toward the truck. I looked at Jason. His mouth was hanging open. Maybe mine did too. We closed them quickly, as soon as Enright turned to us.

"That's it! Two bags. What's in them?" He pulled the two tote bags out of the trunk. There was no black plastic bag. It had simply vanished. I looked at Chris Meagher, who was doing his best to look surprised himself.

Enright searched both bags. It would be more accurate to say he pulled all the clothes out of them and left the contents strewn all over the roadside. "I don't get it. Why all this fuss over a few clothes?"

"It's the principle," I said again.

He stood up, staring all around him. He was thoroughly pissed by the whole affair, and when a policeman is mad, someone has to pay. There is always a crime around somewhere, some law that has been broken.

That was when he spotted the black plastic bag. It hadn't vanished after all, but somehow transported itself, by magic, to a comfortable spot next to a garbage can on the sidewalk. "Look at this," said Enright, disgusted. "Can you believe it? People are told over and over and over again, don't leave rubbish on the sidewalk like this for the dogs to rip open. Honestly, the mess. People have no consideration."

He walked over to the bag and picked it up. "Bloody disgrace," he muttered as he lifted the lid of the garbage can to put the plastic bag inside. But he was frustrated here, too. The lid was already resting on another bulging garbage bag. The bag of marijuana was simply too big and bulky. The lid wouldn't rest on top of it, but fell back loudly against the body of the bin, and the black bag itself kept rolling off. Each time it hit the ground, I held my breath, expecting it to split open.

"Shit!" Enright exploded when the bag fell off a third time. The poor man looked a bit defeated. Not his day, obviously.

Chris Meagher stepped forward. "You're right," he said. "I see rubbish like this all over the place. A disgrace, just like you said, Constable. Look, Rosie," he said, turning to me. "If you're so full of principle, then you should help out. You can take that bag up to the industrial bin behind Jimmy Way's." He pointed toward the Chinese restaurant farther along Hedges Avenue.

Enright saw his chance for a little revenge against me. "Good point," he said, brightening up a little. "Are you going to be a civic-minded citizen and get rid of this bag for me?"

"Of course she will," said Chris. "Only sounds fair, if you ask me, after all the trouble she's caused."

He took the bag from where it had fallen for the third time, strode right past Constable Enright and placed it in the trunk of the Mercedes. Meanwhile, Jason had managed to gather his mate's clothes, along with a lot of dirt and stones, into the tote bags. He dumped these into the trunk as well, and I closed it up with a deep sense of relief.

"Say hello to Paddy for me when you see him," Enright called as he returned to his car. He was sneering as he said it—his idea of a parting insult. Then he left in a shower of dust and grit, spinning his wheels in the gravel.

Jason and I stood watching him go, and only when the police car was out of sight along the tree-lined avenue did we turn back to Chris.

How had he done it? He certainly hadn't sprung the lock. That would have been too risky, and if Enright had seen him from the gate he would have been in more trouble than we were.

Chris smiled and shook his head, rustling those curls. Oh boy. I went weak in the knees. He pulled a socket wrench from his back pocket and held it up while, with his other hand, he invited us to peer into the car itself.

"I can't see anything different," said Jason.

Chris leaned in through the back door and pushed at the seat. It collapsed suddenly as though it had been balancing precariously in place. In fact, it had been. The bolts were on the floor.

"I still don't get it," I said.

Chris leaned in even farther, pulled away the upright section of seat and poked his arm well into the space behind it, right into the trunk. He had found a way into the trunk without opening it with the key!

While Jason and I watched, he bolted both halves of the seat back into place. Good with his hands, Mr. Ferguson had said, and that was easy to see (though I could probably think of a few better things he could do with them). By the time he was finished, guess who was also standing beside us. Ben. That's Ben, the invisible man.

"Where the hell did you go?"

He pointed into the garden two houses up from the fence. "Were my eyes playing tricks, or did that copper really let you put my stash back into the trunk?"

"Sure did," said Jason, and the two of them exploded with laughter.

I kicked them both, Jason first, because he was my brother and he had known all along what was in that bag, then Ben, because it was his stuff and he'd run away and left me to take the rap. Both withdrew strategically to the sidewalk to see if I would attack again. That left me with Chris Meagher. "I guess I owe you a big thank-you."

"No. It's all right. Hey, you're one cool chick, I'll give you that. Did you really throw your keys over that fence?"

"I guess I did."

He whistled in admiration.

I basked in his admiration.

"Look, I was rude to you yesterday when you came for gas. Stared at you like you were some kind of walking centerfold. We don't get many beautiful women around Fergo's."

Not a bad line. But it wasn't going to work. I'd made a promise to Glenda, hadn't I?

"I hope I've evened up the score a bit." He nodded toward the trunk.

Yes, I thought. You *have* redeemed yourself. Though the gas station debacle was really my fault, and he didn't really have anything to apologize for.

"I'd like to make it up to you even more, if it's all right with you. We should see a movie together sometime. What do you say?"

No chance. I'd made that promise to Glenda. She was my leash in case I went getting myself into danger. (Woof, woof.)

I looked at Chris—that face, those curls, and the

gentle, friendly kind of way he was smiling at me, Rosie Sinclair.

Ah, but there was my promise to Glenda. When you make a promise to your best bud, you should stick to it, eh.

Count to three. Time to make up my mind. Say no, Rosie, say no. Tongue up against the top of the mouth to make an "n," then lips pushed out in a little "o." It was like Glenda was standing there, coaching me.

But she wasn't there, was she, and what did Glenda know anyway. "Yeah, okay," I said.

He didn't look surprised, but I didn't care. My head was spinning. "I was going to ring you anyway, to apologize," he said. "I'll call you tonight. Is that all right?"

The arrogance was gone, the teasing smirk of yesterday replaced by a sincerity that reminded me of Todd Rooney. I'd told Glenda that there wasn't enough spark with Todd. Now that Chris was staring down at me, genuinely pleased at what he found, there was more than just a spark. You could have shoved me in a fireplace and toasted marshmallows on my skin.

Jason and Ben ventured off the sidewalk. "Listen, Rosie," my brother called. "We're sorry about all this. But look, it's over now and we've still got the dope."

I turned to face them. Yes, I still had the dope, in the trunk of my black taxi. I climbed into the driver's seat and started up the Mercedes while the two guys went around to shake Chris's hand and thank him. Perfect timing.

I planted my foot on the accelerator and took off up the road. Vague shouts of, "Hey, Rosie, what the hell . . ." reached my ears until I was out of range.

I didn't go straight home. There was the question of that black plastic bag to take care of. If I gave it back to Ben, he would only get in trouble again, and Jason along with him. Someone had to look out for my brain-dead brother.

Once I was out of sight, I started looking for somewhere to dump the bag. Chris had already mentioned Jimmy Way's, so I couldn't take it there. Ah, just the place. There was an open Dumpster on the sidewalk in front of a building site. I tossed in the plastic bag and slipped a discarded sheet of plasterboard over the top.

Then I went home, wondering how I could keep the truth from Glenda.

THIRTEEN

To make sure I didn't get into any more trouble with my cell phone at school, I now left it in the glove box and checked my voice mail after school. This was the first message I had received on Thursday:

Rosie.

A hesitation.

Rosie? Rosie?

Pause.

Oh, you have one of those damn machines. A curse, if you ask me.

Lengthy silence.

Umm, I need a lift . . . er, my sister. Oh, I can't think when there's no one there listening.

Mrs. Foat hung up.

This was the second message:

Listen up, girl. I've heard about Paddy and why he's not answering his phone. It makes no difference to me who's driving that black heap of junk. I want the ring.

And remember this, too. Your grandfather's in jail, right. That's a very nasty place to be if you annoy the wrong people. I've got friends in low places, if you get my meaning. Cough up what I'm after or your grandad's going to have a little accident.

For a moment, I was about to cry, then told myself not to be such a girl. But the voice had threatened Grandad now, and he was so vulnerable there in jail. I saw him in my mind, the way he looked when we had gone to see him last weekend. The prison uniform, the long face. I *had* to find the stupid ring that this horrible man was so eager to get his hands on. It wasn't in the car. Glenda and I had searched it, and I'd had two more goes by myself, even under the hood, to see if it was hooked over a spark plug lead, anything. No sign of it.

If I couldn't find the ring, I had to try and work out who might be making the threats. Glenda had done all she could. There was only one place I could find out more, distasteful though it was. I had to speak to Uncle Bruce.

He had a favorite watering hole called Ritt's Hotel. That's right. I haven't got the name wrong. A guy named Freddy Ritt had come up with the clever idea of naming a hotel after himself in the hope that people would think it had some connection to the famous swanky place in London. Ha! Some hope. It was the biggest dive in Prestwidge.

I parked the Mercedes under the only light in the

parking lot that hadn't been smashed, crossing my fingers that the light would deter thieves. Better be quick, I told myself. I marched straight in through the front door, making a few heads turn, but no one challenged me. There was Bruce Larkin, on a stool, with his back to me, holding up the bar.

"I want to talk to you," I announced before he even knew I was behind him.

He hunched his shoulders and put his hands over his head as though he expected to be banged on the noggin. When nothing hit him, he turned around. "Shit! Rosie, you gave me a fright. What are you doing here?"

"I want to know what's going on. Some ring's gone missing and people think Grandad's got it."

"Hey, keep your voice down," he said, staring around wildly, but no one was paying the least attention.

"Don't try to deny it. You were searching for it when I found you in Grandad's car."

To my surprise, he admitted as much without an argument. "How did you find out?"

I told him about the sinister phone calls. He let out a worried sigh. "Word's getting around, then."

"What's so special about this ring anyway?"

"What's so special! It's worth twenty thousand dollars, that's what."

"Shit!" Even I was impressed, not that I gave a damn really. It was Grandad's safety that concerned me. I turned the tables on Bruce. "So how did you know to look in the Mercedes?"

His head ducked first to one side, then to the other, before he drew me in close. "Look, no one knows for sure. It's all a bit of guesswork, but I've got this mate, right, and he's passed on the word that's doing the rounds. A bloke named McWhirter tried to knock over this jewelry store, going back a few weeks ago. A proper lowlife, really and completely useless. Everyone is surprised he dared to have a go at this place. Anyway, he ended up in the hospital."

"I know about this," I said. "He's in a coma."

"Not anymore, he's not."

That was a surprise. Obviously Bruce's sources were better than Glenda's and mine. "Well, if he's awake, the police must be all over him with their questions," I murmured. "But all the jewelry was recovered, except for this ring that's supposed to be in the Mercedes. Did this McWhirter bloke say he hid it in Grandad's car? Is that what all this fuss is about?"

"No. If he'd told the police that, they would have impounded the car by now. No, the word is, McWhirter can't remember a thing. His brain didn't work so well at the best of times, but now it's like scrambled eggs. That's what the doctors reckon up at the hospital, so McWhirter's not scamming. It's for real."

"But what's the connection with Grandad's car?"

"I'm only guessing, like I said, but it makes sense to

me. Trouble is, it looks like I'm not the only one who's worked it out."

"What are you talking about? Worked *what* out?"

"The car," he hissed, doing another check to make sure no one was listening, but frankly, if there was anyone in the bar who gave two hoots, I couldn't spot him. "It's because of where Paddy left his car on the night of the jewel robbery."

"It was outside his mate's place. The one who owned the van."

"George Goggin," Bruce reminded me. "But it's where GG lives that's the point."

I still didn't have a clue.

"He lives in a little lane off Gresham Street," Bruce tried to explain, and at last I had a name that made a connection.

"Gresham Street. That's where the jewelry store is!"

"Farr's," he said nodding. "Farr's Fine Jewelry. That's the place McWhirter tried to turn over, only it all went wrong. Someone saw his flashlight and rang the cops. Sirens everywhere. He ditched a packet of gemstones on an empty block, but for some reason he wanted a better hiding spot for the ring."

"Grandad's Mercedes."

"Ah, *now* you get it. Everyone in Prestwidge knows Paddy Larkin's car, and there it was, parked in the street. McWhirter knows if he's caught with the ring on him, he'll end up in jail, but if he hides it somewhere that no one would think of looking—"

I beat him to the rest. "Somewhere he can get it back from, anytime he likes. But doesn't it take time to break into a car?"

Bruce made a rude, dismissive noise through his lips. "Not if you know what you're doing," he said in a tone that showed *he* certainly did, and I didn't. "That McWhirter was stealing cars before his voice broke. Would have been in and out again in ten seconds flat."

"So he hides the ring somewhere in the Mercedes, then walks off down the street like he's out for a night-time stroll, then gets hit by a drunk on a bicycle. Meanwhile, poor Grandad runs into the police, they search the van and find those parkas, and now *he's* in jail instead." (Instead of *you*, I almost added.)

"Dumb bad luck," said Bruce as though he were pronouncing fate's verdict from on high.

"But why didn't the police think of all this and come looking for the ring?"

"The police!" he said with disdain. "They couldn't find their own arseholes with a sniffer dog."

"So who do you think is making those calls to Grandad's phone?"

"Could be anyone. Twenty thousand dollars is a lot of money."

"What's a jewelry store in Prestwidge doing with a ring like that, anyway?"

114

"Wasn't for sale. Belongs to Terry Sidebottom, or his wife, at least. Engagement ring."

I'd heard of Mr. Sidebottom. His name was always turning up in the local newspaper along with a picture of his sweating, bloated face. He was a big name in real estate. Everywhere you looked you'd see a sign advertising Prestwidge Land and Housing with his name along the bottom.

"What was it doing in the shop?"

"Being fixed, apparently. That's how they know what it's worth. Terry wanted it valued while it was in for repairs. He's offered a reward, you know. Three thousand dollars. Wants it back for his wife, eh. Sentimental value or something." He laughed bitterly to himself. "Sentiment. That's a good one. Terry Sidebottom's a ruthless bastard. Memory or no memory, I wouldn't like to be McWhirter once he gets out of the hospital." This brought a brief chuckle, then the smile disappeared. "That's what makes these threats on the phone a bit of a worry, Rosie. Everyone knows Sidebottom's reputation. If a bloke's willing to risk getting hold of that ring, considering who it belongs to, then he's sure to be just as ruthless. We're talking a serious criminal here."

Suddenly, I needed a drink, something to stop my mouth from drying out altogether.

"Rosie," Bruce said in a whisper, "you haven't got it, have you?"

I was distracted by my fears for Grandad. "Got what?"

"The ring, of course."

I looked at him like he was something stuck on the sole of my shoe. "Why would I have listened to all this if I already had the damn thing?"

"All right. I was just asking. But if you *did* have it, the best thing would be to give it to me, right?"

Slimeball, I thought to myself. There's his own father in danger of having an "accident" in jail and he just wants the reward. That's why he asked me. What would that creep on the phone do to Grandad if he found out we'd handed the ring back to the owners? I didn't even want to think about it.

I went home and searched the car all over again, more thoroughly than ever this time.

Zilch, zippo! A big fat zero! That story Uncle Bruce had come up with to explain the interest in the Mercedes might sound plausible, but if the ring had ever been in Grandad's car, it certainly wasn't there now.

My day ended on a better note, at least. Chris rang after I had been home an hour or so and asked me to the movies on Saturday night. That was fine for a first date; I wouldn't have to meet a lot of his friends at some party where everyone got off their faces. This would be just me and him. Perfect.

FOURTEEN

The next day was Friday—and even better than that, it was the last day of school before a week-long holiday! I honored a long-standing tradition among Prestwidge seniors and took the day off. Mental health day, I told myself and I was serious. I had errands for my old people banked up like a freeway at rush hour, and with that threat hanging over Grandad's head, how could I sit in class taking *anything* in? Besides, that dreaded voice had promised to ring back, and this time I had to speak to him, direct. I could hardly sit in the classroom waiting for him to call, could I?

I spent the morning catching up with the backlog of short trips around Prestwidge, with the cell phone on the front seat beside me. Every time it rang, I jumped. At this rate, I'd have an accident soon.

Mrs. Foat finally got ahold of me in person. I picked her up and delivered her to the hospital, and since I had taken care of the other jobs by then, I even went up with her to the third floor to see her sister. She was even farther away with the pixies now, poor thing. (I don't want to grow old. I wonder if you can get an exemption, like missing out on P.E. at school.)

Fortunately, Mrs. Foat did all the talking. "It's a lovely day outside, Meredith. My geraniums are doing well. Got to be careful I don't overwater them." Whether her sister took in a single word was hard to tell. After a while, I left them both there and went for a walk. Good for my problem area. Tones it up.

So far there had been no word from the Voice of the Underworld. Did he know I was sweating on his call? Was he following me, watching me become more and more nervous? I looked around, examining every face, near and far. The bastard. Now he'd made me completely paranoid.

It was time to fetch Mrs. Foat and take her home when the phone rang again. Oh, God. Was it him? What was I going to say?

"Rosie. It's Glenda."

"Oh hi!" I said, letting out a relieved sigh.

"Don't you 'hi' me, you lying cow."

Oh dear. "Cow" was very high on Glenda's list of unaffectionate terms. I could guess what was coming, but how had she found out?

"What are you talking about?" I said, bluffing shamelessly.

"Don't," she spluttered. "Just don't go on with the

innocent act, right. You're going out with Chris Meagher after all, aren't you? Don't deny it. I heard it from a girl who buys her joints from a half-wit named Ben who's mates with your half-witted brother."

I tried to explain how Chris had gallantly rescued me from a life behind bars, but she wouldn't listen. "I need a lift home from school, *now*. Come and get me."

That was a command, not a request. Unfortunately, I couldn't fetch Mrs. Foat from the hospital and drive her home without leaving Glenda stranded for an hour. "Do you mind if I pick up a friend before I take you home?" I asked Mrs. Foat when I got back to the hospital.

"Not at all. I'd enjoy a little drive." She settled into the backseat as though this were a Sunday outing.

She was so quiet and unnoticeable that when I picked up Glenda she didn't even realize my elderly passenger was there. As soon as she had slammed the door shut, she launched into me. "I warned you, didn't I? You're out of your depth. He's twenty-one years old. Why you don't just go out with Todd Rooney I can't understand."

We went over the same ground we had covered in her bedroom a few days before. Or at least she did. I just listened, wishing I had a half bar of mint chocolate. Glenda still hadn't seen Mrs. Foat. I glanced over my shoulder and found the old dear staring out the window as though she hadn't heard a word.

Glenda saw me staring and finally turned around.

"Oh shit!" she exclaimed.

Mrs. Foat pretended she hadn't heard all over again while Glenda apologized. I thought it was time I introduced them.

At least this interlude had put a sock in Glenda's mouth. Now I had a chance to respond. "I tried to explain the other day," I insisted. "Todd's a nice boy and does everything sweetly and he's good-looking and I must say there is a bit of attraction there." Plus it makes the girls at school insanely jealous! "But with Chris, well, I don't know what it is. I want to find out, so I know what it is about him that just makes me feel . . ." I shrugged and looked a bit helpless, which wasn't the right thing to do in front of Glenda at that moment.

She craned her neck for another gander at Mrs. Foat, who had rolled the window down a little to let the breeze play in her wispy gray hair. "It's sex isn't it, Rosie," said Glenda, as softly as she could.

"No, of course not!" I scolded her. I was scandalized. "Honestly, that's not it at all." It was the truth—at least I was pretty sure it was. (Bloody hormones!) I had only just met him. Barely spoken to him really, and I wasn't that kind of girl, as Glenda knew only too well, being my best friend.

She gave me that older sister look. "This is the classic dilemma and you're hardly the first girl who's been there. Nice boy versus dangerous brute. You're attracted to

Chris because he's someone you know you shouldn't go anywhere near."

"What, a couple of semesters of psychology and you know all about it, do you?"

"This is nothing to do with psychology. This is real life. You can still call off the date, you know."

"No, I can't do that. I'd be too embarrassed."

"No problem. I'll ring him for you. I'll tell him you're washing your hair or something."

"Don't you dare. Oh, Glenda. Do you really think he's no good for me?"

"YES," she said with a Paddy Larkin firmness that unnerved me. I stopped arguing, so that she would stop trying to convince me. I was sort of half convinced she was right, even though I didn't want to be. Oh God, what should I do?

I dropped Glenda at her place and continued on toward Mrs. Foat's house. "I'm sorry about all these detours," I said.

"Not at all, Rosie. I've quite enjoyed myself."

From her tone, I suspected she wasn't just talking about the ride. "I hope we didn't shock you with all that girl talk."

"Shock me? Oh, goodness no. I must confess to you, Rosie, I listened to every word."

She was smiling openly now. "You two are just like me and my girlfriends from years ago. Good to see you modern ones still talk about the same things. I was worried the hairy-legged crowd and the bra burners had banished all that liveliness out of you young things."

I wasn't sure who she was talking about. I wasn't into shaving my legs too often myself, but that stuff about bras sounded decidedly off.

"You never forget, you know," she said whimsically, still with the wind in her hair. "For me, it was a boy named Colin. Oh, he was a wild one. I used to go weak in the knees every time I saw him. He noticed me, too, I made sure of that." She latched on to some memory that sent her cheeks a healthy pink. Then she leaned forward on the seat and urged in a half whisper, "Don't let your friend talk you out of it, Rosie. There's plenty of time to be safe, and it's a long life to live without a bit of passion to remember on those lonely nights."

I remembered the photos I'd seen at her house. "Your husband," I said cautiously. "His name wasn't Colin, was it?"

"No, dear. It was Geoffrey."

We rode on in silence for almost a minute and then, "Go for the dangerous one, girl," she said.

And that's how it happened that Mrs. Foat of all people helped me make up my mind.

When I arrived home, the creature on the sofa showed signs of life and eventually spoke. He didn't seem to harbor any grudge that I had left him stranded on Hedges

Avenue. "There was a call for you," he announced list-lessly. "Some guy. Number's on the pad beside the phone."

At last Jason had found useful employment. He was an answering machine.

"Did he say his name?"

"Yeah."

Silence followed. I'd better retract that last statement about my brother. At least an answering machine would repeat the full message, and usually you could tell who was calling from the sound of the voice.

"Well?"

"I'm thinking."

I wondered what the strange noise was.

"Was it Chris?"

"No," he said uncertainly. "Ted or something like that."

"Todd."

"Yeah, that was it." Jason found a half-finished biscuit among the blankets, which seemed to please him. Now he wouldn't have to go to the kitchen for something to eat.

I took the cordless phone into my bedroom and rang Todd Rooney.

"Oh, hi, Rosie. Thanks for calling back," he said.

"Sorry I wasn't here when you called."

"No worries," he said cheerfully. "I tried to get you a couple of times last week, but you're hardly at home. Have you got a cell phone?"

"It's not working," I lied. "There's something wrong with the battery and I have to keep it turned off a lot of the time."

He didn't seem to mind. In fact, he started talking as though it were only yesterday that we'd been to that party. He was easy to listen to and I just lay back on the bed, laughing at some of the things he said about his parents. He was a nice guy, no doubt about that.

Then Todd came to the point. "Listen, Rosie. We had a great night when we went out. Want to do it again sometime?"

"Yeah, sure," I said before I'd thought about it.

"Cool." I could just see his smile at the other end of the line. "I was thinking of tomorrow night, actually. Just you and me this time."

Tomorrow night! Think quickly. I realized suddenly that despite everything I had said to Glenda, I would quite like to go out with Todd again. But tomorrow night I was going to the movies with Chris Meagher, and I wasn't about to break my date with him. (It wasn't just me now. I had to keep faith with Mrs. Foat, didn't I?)

I was very careful about the next sounds I made, trying for that perfect mixture of disappointment and regret. "Oh, Todd, I'm sorry. I can't. Not tomorrow night." *Insert excuse here*. But *what* excuse? I hadn't thought of one yet. There was no time to work on different options. My tongue just kept moving, hoping that my brain would send down the signal in time.

"I've got to baby-sit." Phew! Give yourself a high five, girl! "I can't get out of it either. The lady booked me up to do it more than a week ago, and she rang me again just now to confirm, so I can't let her down."

He sounded heartbroken, but took it well. "I'll organize something else, then. Another night."

"Yes. I'd like that." We talked a bit more and then he had to go, still sounding disappointed. "Rosie Sinclair," I said out loud. "You want to have your cake and eat it too."

Cake is for wimps. I needed chocolate.

Mum was home by this time. "We're out of milk," I lied. "I'd better go up to the corner store and get some. Can I have some money?" This was an old scam I'd learned in primary school as a way of supplementing my limited supplies of cash. Mum couldn't be bothered handing out coins from her purse and always gave me bills instead. Never remembered to ask for the change. This time she handed over a ten-dollar bill.

At the store, I grabbed a carton of milk and went looking for the chocolate. Actually, I could hear it calling to me from three aisles away, *Rosie, Rosie*, and there it was, the strongest calls coming from a large bar with rows of soft mint centers.

No, I told myself severely, a whole family-sized bar would be indulgent, an absolute extravagance, even if I had the money, which I did. Not to mention what it would do to my problem area. But this was a major drama I had to get over, here. Two-timing boys was not something I had ever done before. Then there was that stuff that Glenda wouldn't tell me about her relationship with Chris a couple of years ago, and I hadn't even dared think about that yet.

What the heck. I bought the largest size and ate two rows in the car on the way home. The guilt became unbearable, which meant I needed someone to chew me out. Glenda seemed the best choice and I knew she wouldn't have turned into Giselle just yet, so I gave her a call on the cell phone.

"You turned down a date with Todd Rooney! That's a crime," she exploded down the line at me. "Listen, girl-friend, those hormones of yours will end up with a crim-inal record." Of course, she didn't know that I had another date instead. She scolded me for another five minutes, then stopped abruptly. "What's that smacking sound?"

"What sound?"

"In my ear. It's been going on ever since you called me. You're eating something."

"No."

"Don't lie to me, Rosie. It's chocolate. Mint centers. I can smell it it from here."

"Glenda, we're on the phone."

"Doesn't matter. I know you. What size bar did you get?"

"The smallest one. Snack size."

"It's a big bar, isn't it."

"No."

"How much is left?"

I looked down at the silver wrapping paper. "Not a lot."

"You're hopeless, honestly. Save the rest for me."

I did. (Well, I saved her the last row.)

FIFTEEN

On Saturday, all the old people of Prestwidge must have found someone else to be their taxi because they left me alone all day to worry about my date with Chris Meagher.

The eternal question: what to wear? Under the circumstances, my access to Glenda's wardrobe seemed cut off for the time being, and the one thing of hers that I did have, the little black skirt, was attached to that scene at the gas station, which I'd rather forget. Nothing in my closet. Time to shop.

There was a fabulous skirt in Rags for Ragers that I'd had my eye on for weeks. It was red, with gold embroidery just above the hem. I'd tried it on so many times the sales assistant couldn't be bothered getting her hopes up when I turned up yet again to check it out. Way too expensive, of course. It would empty my humble bank account completely, but without Glenda along to act as my good sense, I bought it anyway.

And now, the top . . . What top could possibly match my new skirt? No chance of buying a new one. I went through my wardrobe. Flick, no; flick, no, can't wear pink with red. There was a nice white one, but it had tacky silver spangles dusted over the bust. *So* passé. God, what was I thinking when I bought it? On I went. Flick, no; flick, no; flick, *stop*. There it was. Black would go perfectly with my new skirt. But the neckline! Somehow I had found the courage to buy it, but I had never dared to wear it.

I took it off the hanger. (Thank God for hormones.) If the A-list could see me now, they would put blindfolds on their boyfriends, then beg me for fashion tips. For a few moments I indulged in this pleasing fantasy. No, I decided, I don't need Justine's or Clare's or Fiona's approval. Plunging neckline or not, Rosie was still Rosie.

Chris had said seven o'clock. At seven thirty there was still no sign of him. Glenda has a rule. If they are more than twenty minutes late, the date is off, which just goes to show she has never been desperate to go out with any one guy. But he might have had the courtesy to ring and say he would be late. Frown, grumble. I tried watching some mindless TV with the resident zombie for a while to distract me. I had to keep turning away every time Mum walked into the room, in case she saw my top and went berserk.

At a quarter to eight, a car finally pulled up outside, and I hurried out the front door and down the path so he wouldn't have to come in and see Jason on the couch, or worse, meet my mother. I was a bit disappointed to see that the car was actually the same truck Chris had been driving when he rescued me from Constable Enright. It sported mag wheels and a fox's tail on the tip of the antenna. A typical Prestiemobile. What the hell, I'm a typical Prestie chick.

He climbed out of the car and watched me pick my way through the cracked concrete of our front path in my ridiculously high heels. "Hi!" he called brightly as he walked round to the curb. No apology for being forty-five minutes late. "Hey, you look great."

I forgot about apologies. Every cent I'd spent on the skirt had been worth it, and so had the hour and twenty minutes I'd spent in front of the mirror getting my make-up right. Chris opened the door for me and I slipped into the seat. At least I tried to. My bottom just kept going down until it couldn't go any farther. The halt was rather sudden. More than that, it was painful. "Ouch," I cried.

I pulled myself up quickly and heard an ominous rip. "Oh, shit, no," I swore, which wasn't very ladylike, but even the queen of England would have said something rude if she'd heard that sound. "My skirt!"

I was out on the sidewalk again by now, contorting my body like a dog trying to catch its tail so I could see what had happened to my brand-new skirt. In the end, I had to loosen it at the waist and turn it round ninety degrees, which isn't something you do in front of a boy on the first date if you can avoid it. There it was, a rip in the material.

"Not too big," said Chris soothingly.

"Not too big!" I repeated, keeping my voice to a low shout. "It might as well be a foot wide." In fact, it was closer to half an inch, but the skirt was still ruined.

"Must be a spring. This is Darren's truck and hardly anyone sits in that seat. Just his dog, mainly."

"Oh, thanks. That makes me feel much better. Where's *your* car?"

"Still up on the lift at Fergo's. That's why I'm late. Couldn't get the new muffler fitted in time."

Still no apology, but at least there was an excuse. I angrily straightened my skirt. "Damn. I got this from Rags for Ragers just this morning."

"Don't worry about it," he said, as though I was making a fuss about nothing. "I'll get something to put over the spring."

While I tossed up whether to go back inside and change, he threw back the tarpaulin that covered the back of Darren's truck and rummaged around in the darkness. I decided to stay put, mainly because there was nothing in my wardrobe that looked half decent and besides, if I went inside now, Mum would want to know why, and it would all be a hundred times more embarrassing than it already was. *Not* a good start.

It didn't get any better when Chris pulled out a piece of cardboard. "Here, this should do the trick."

"I can't sit on that. It's filthy."

He looked at it more closely. "Yeah, s'pose it is." He went back to looking.

"I've got a better idea. We can go in the Mercedes."

He stopped his hopeful rummaging about under the tarp and stood looking at me.

"Yeah, all right," he answered. "I love those old cars. So well built."

Just like you, I thought to myself. We walked to the car, both of us arriving at the driver's door together. He had his hand out for the keys.

"Sorry, Chris. This is my grandad's car. I can't let anyone else drive it. It was a promise I made to him."

Technically this was a lie. It was only certain members of the family who were disqualified, like Uncle Bruce and Mum and Jason and Grandma—all the family, come to think of it—but I wasn't giving up those keys to Chris, either.

"Come on, Rosie. Girls don't drive. It's the guy's job, especially when I'm taking you out."

I made a face that said there was nothing I could do about it. He sighed and walked round to the passenger's side, climbed in and folded his arms rather sullenly. This wasn't going the way either of us had planned.

It got worse.

I drove out onto Hedges Avenue, then turned onto the Promenade, which swept grandly down to the mall. The Promenade is a four-lane road with two lanes in each direction. I was cruising just at the speed limit when a car swept up beside us, in a hurry to get somewhere. It was a big, ugly sedan that purred with the deep rumbling sounds of a V-8 engine. Chris turned instinctively to look at it.

"Oh great," he sighed when he saw the occupants. Typical Presties with mullet haircuts and flannels. These two guys wore sunglasses and looked like they'd seen too many Quentin Tarantino movies. The driver had his window down and his arm resting halfway out the door. "Hey Meagher. That's you, isn't it? Lost your license, have you, mate?"

Chris ignored them, but I could see he wasn't happy.

"Just as well you've got a chick to do the driving for you then, eh."

Chris rolled up the window but by then they had lost interest. The driver put the pedal to the metal and they roared off.

My dream date didn't say a word. I thought it best to do the same. Maybe we should have turned around, gone home, started all over again, pretended my skirt wasn't ripped. Maybe I should even have let him drive Grandad's car. We didn't do any of these things, hoping it would all get better, but sometimes the planets are just aligned the wrong way in the sky. As I stood beside Chris in the line to buy our tickets, I saw a face staring at me. It was Todd Rooney.

He came over. "Hi, Rosie," he said with a look on

his face I couldn't read. "This is the baby you had to mind, is it?"

I deserved that.

Chris didn't know what was going on, but he sensed the sarcasm in Todd's voice. "Hey, sonny boy. Watch the way you talk to Rosie, or I'll rearrange your pretty face."

That would have been just perfect, a fight between Todd and Chris, but Todd wasn't interested in a fight, and he knew he would get pummelled anyway. He backed away to join his mates.

Chris and I sat through the movie like two people who didn't know each other. Since my mind was locked into Worry and Disaster mode, it tortured me with images of Grandad being roughed up by a bunch of thugs in jail. I couldn't get them out of my head.

"Do you want to go for coffee?" Chris asked me afterward.

I could tell from the tone of his voice that he was hoping I'd say no.

"Sorry, I'm tired."

I drove home. On the sidewalk beside Darren's truck, we stood together, not daring to look at each other. "I'm really sorry, Rosie. I was looking forward to tonight. You're very pretty, you know." Then he leaned across and pecked me on the cheek. "Good night."

What a disaster. Could it have been any worse? I went into my bedroom and just lay there in the dark with my hand over my face. I was touching the skin of my cheek, where he'd kissed me, ever so lightly. Despite everything, it burned.

How could it have all gone so wrong, so quickly? I know he likes me. There's a kind of light in his eyes when he looks at me. It was there when he first turned up tonight and I swear I could see it again when he told me how pretty I was and he gave me that peck on the cheek.

I wished I could talk to Glenda about it. There was my bag on the edge of the bed, with the cell phone inside. I fished it out, but there was no point. She was being Giselle tonight and wouldn't get home until about five in the morning. She needed to sleep when she did make it home, so I couldn't ring until the afternoon. Even if I could catch her between shows at the club, I was in for a huge slice of "I told you so."

My room was dark and cold and lonely, just like my mood. I couldn't be bothered getting undressed, so I simply pulled a blanket over myself and kicked my shoes out from under it. They landed with a heavy thud, one, then the other, on the floor. Sounded like my heart sinking. Come on sleep, I thought, make it all go away.

As soon as I started to drift off, a new worry crept into my head. How was I going to get gas for the Merc without seeing Chris? I drifted into half sleep again. Then a phone was ringing far away. I wished Mum would answer it, because it was keeping me back from that last step down the ladder into a deep sleep. Come on, Mum, answer it. It was a familiar ring, one that I just couldn't ignore. Like Grandad's cell phone. Yeah, a bit like that. Silly tune.

It *was* Grandad's cell phone! I wrenched myself quickly out of sleep. Where was it? The sound was muffled because the phone had become tangled in the bedclothes. At last I found it and felt for the big Answer button, hoping despite myself that I would hear Glenda's voice when I put it to my ear.

"Are you ready to hand over that ring yet, girlie?" said a voice that was becoming all too familiar.

It was the "girlie" part that did it. If he had just said "girl" I might have stayed calm. But "girlie"! Who did he think he was? I was fed up with this rude mongrel and I told him so. "I'm fed up with you, you rude mongrel," I shouted into the phone. For a few seconds, it didn't matter who he was or what he wanted, I went for him. All the fear and the frustration and the tension I'd felt in my shoulders these last few days was because of him. "Look, buster," I said bluntly. "I'm sick of you ringing me up at whatever time it suits you, making threats about my grandad. I haven't got the stupid ring from that robbery. Do you understand that? NOT-HERE. SOME-WHERE-ELSE. Do I have to draw you a map? It's not in the car. I've been over it from one end to the other five times."

Wow, I even surprised myself. To tell you the truth, I think the failure of my dream date with Chris might have had something to do with it. Before he could speak, I was at him again. "I'm sick of hearing about that ring. Do you hear me? I don't care what it's worth or whether there's a reward or if you're some big-time criminal. You know what I'd do, if I did have it? I wouldn't give it to you, that's for sure. I'd . . . I'd take it to the police."

There was an odd silence. I don't know quite what I expected, but I heard a sudden intake of breath coming down the line. In each of the calls I'd had from this horrible man, he had lorded it over me completely, yet here was a moment of vulnerability that I couldn't understand. What had I said?

But it seems I had misread that silence badly. He was just gathering himself to return my anger with interest. "Now, you listen to me. If you're one of Larkin's brood then you're no doubt a thief like him. You're holding out on me, going right to the edge same as any thief would, hoping I'll just go away and you can have that ring for yourself. Well, it won't work with me, understand? I want that ring in my hands and no one else's. If you take it anywhere near the police, it's Paddy who'll pay the price. Do you understand me? Maybe I should make it a bit clearer. Have you seen the heavy doors they've got in that jail? Very dangerous, those doors. You have to watch where you put your hands, especially around the hinges. People have been known to lose a finger or two in those doors."

I cringed at the thought. I couldn't help it. I even bent my own fingers, opening and closing them over my palm in reaction. "Please . . . ," I whimpered pathetically.

It was what he wanted to hear, I think, because he eased up and became more businesslike. "I'll call again and make arrangements to get the ring, and if by any chance you're telling the truth and you haven't found it yet, you'd better get looking. Remember, as soon as that ring is in my hands, your grandad's suddenly a very safe man."

SIXTEEN

On Sunday, I had a long-standing engagement. Normally, when my old people needed to go somewhere, they rang up and expected me to be there straightaway, like I was a taxi. But this gig was arranged beforehand. Mrs. Duval was going to bingo.

It was Mr. Duval who rang me on Friday, just to make sure I hadn't forgotten. I'd heard how old people have their little rituals, and if they get disrupted it can upset them for days afterward. I assured the dear old thing that I wouldn't let his wife down.

So, after a night spent worrying about Grandad, the hole in my skirt, and most of all, the huge hole in my heart, I pulled up outside the Duvals' house at a few minutes to ten. They welcomed me like I was *their* granddaughter, not Paddy's. Janice was well dressed for the occasion in a soft pastel twin-set and pleated skirt. "Those heels are a bit high," I commented, then bit my tongue. For a second, I'd sounded like my mother—

"You can't go out in that." All the same, I was surprised. I mean, Mrs. D sometimes needed a hand on the stairs, and though these shoes only had heels an inch high, if she went over in them, she'd break her ankle for sure. But then, bingo is a big thing with some people, I gather, and most of the players would be old dears like herself. It was her chance to get out the gladrags and show off a bit.

Eric was bustling about making sure she had everything, her purse to buy cards, the cinnamon cake she'd made yesterday especially for this occasion. He was putting plastic wrap over it as I came in. I thought to myself, I bet he enjoys this little interlude each month. The only time he has the house to himself. I wonder, does he put his feet on the furniture, sit round with his shirt off in front of the TV, drinking beer straight from the bottle and burping like a caveman. They had an ancient stereo, with a turntable instead of a CD player. Maybe he cranked it up and played Frank Sinatra records at full volume. Wow. Boogie time for wrinklies. What a thought.

Mrs. Duval was ready to go. "Where is this bingo hall?" I asked as I was helping her into the Mercedes.

"Downstairs at the RSL," she said.

Now, I knew the RSL pretty well because it was Grandad's favorite watering hole, and the only thing downstairs at the RSL is a parking lot. I pointed this out.

"Not Prestwidge, dear. The Martindale RSL."

"Martindale? That's a long way just to play bingo."

"I have old friends there," she said. "It's how we stay in touch."

Fine with me. I aimed the Merc toward Martindale. Maplethorpe Road was the best way, I decided, almost a freeway at this time on a Sunday morning, but as soon as I turned onto it, I noticed Mrs. D shift in her seat, as though she were about to say something. She was watching me too.

"Rosie," she said finally. "Has Paddy said anything to you about my bingo?"

I shook my head. "I don't get much of a chance to see him, do I?"

"No, of course not. I didn't mean to be insensitive." She fell silent again while the Mercedes ate up another mile.

"Actually, Rosie," she said suddenly, "could you turn left at those lights up ahead?"

"But Martindale's straight on—"

"I've changed my mind," she said. "I might miss bingo for this week. There's a friend of mine who's not terribly well. Perhaps I should pay a visit instead."

This was something of a shock after all the enthusiasm for bingo. I turned left as she commanded and, soon afterward, right onto Hedges Avenue. So I wasn't destined to escape Prestwidge that day, after all. She was becoming excited now, shifting constantly in her seat and keen to show me where to turn off the main road.

In fact, she was downright jittery as she guided me through a few more side streets.

"Is your friend very ill?" I asked. I had Mrs. Foat's sister in mind and wondered whether it would be a bed-side vigil for Janice as well.

She didn't answer. She was concentrating too hard on finding the street. "Here," she said excitedly. "The green house just a few doors along."

I pulled over to the curb and cut the engine.

"I can manage from here, thank you, Rosie," said Mrs. Duval. "You stay in the car."

"Are you sure?" I said, concerned.

"Yes, perfectly sure. Now you'll be back for me at three, won't you?"

I nodded. That was the arrangement, and once I'd dropped her home again, I would go round to Glenda's.

"Oh, here. Don't forget your cinnamon cake," I reminded her.

"You have it, dear," she said, barely turning her head, as though she couldn't care less about it. "It's really your grandfather who likes cinnamon cake."

Well, I knew that, but . . . This was all a bit strange. I watched as Mrs. Duval worked her way out of the Mercedes, and only then did I look up at the house. There was a man standing on the porch, watching her come along the path. Somehow, I had assumed it was a woman she would be visiting. Wait a minute, I thought. This old bloke is expecting her! But how could he have known Mrs. Duval was coming when she herself only changed her mind ten minutes ago? There was something suspicious happening here. If she knew she was going to meet a sick friend, why all that pretense about bingo back at the house?

I watched Mrs. Duval walk along the garden path, beginning to think that *I* was being led along a garden path myself. In the time I'd known her, I'd never seen her walk with as much enthusiasm.

The man came down the three steps from the porch, as though he wanted to take her arm and help her into the house. He took more than her arm. He had his arm around her shoulder as they mounted the steps, then, in the last couple of strides before they disappeared through the door, his arm dropped affectionately to her waist.

The penny finally dropped. I knew what was going on here! At last I'd found out why Grandad wanted me to be discreet. Bingo! Ha! Dear old Mrs. Duval had a boyfriend!

Poor Eric, I thought, as I drove back along Hedges Avenue. The whole thing had been such a shock that I'd had to stop somewhere for a coffee and a think. Discreet? I was *speechless*! The cell phone rang, making me jump. It wouldn't be that horrid man or his henchman, surely.

"Hello?"

"Rosie? It's Eric Duval."

Here was my first chance to practice being discreet. "Oh, hi, Mr. Duval. Is anything the matter?" Butter wouldn't melt in my mouth.

"No, just ringing to see if you got Janice to her bingo all right."

"Yeah, no problem." I cringed.

"Oh, that's good, then." Brief pause. "Listen, Rosie. I wonder, could I impose upon you again, just for a short trip this time? It's really rather important."

I felt so sorry for the guy, I would have driven him right across the country if he had asked. I fired up the Merc and headed off toward the Duval house for the second time that morning. Eric was waiting for me, better dressed now, with his hair done neatly and his leather shoes shining.

"Where to?"

"Oh, a friend of mine rang to ask me over for a drink. I'll show you the way."

He had mentioned this trip was important and somehow I didn't think a drink with an old mate fell quite into that category. But what the heck. He needed a bit of sympathetic handling, even if he didn't realize it.

"Just head onto Hedges Avenue to start with," he told me. I was very conscious of how I had been on this road already this morning and of how discretion meant I couldn't give myself away by saying so. Then Eric pointed to a corner ahead. "Turn up there, if you would."

It was the same place I'd turned off for Mrs. Duval. Just a coincidence, I decided. There was a lot of Prestwidge we could be going to yet. My confidence started to slip mightily, though, when he gave me the next direction. We were definitely following the same route, and if we kept on like this, we'd end up outside that little green house. Butterflies did disgusting things in my stomach. Did he know? Was he making me drive him to that same house to confront the lovers? I couldn't bear to think of the scene that would follow. We were no more than a few streets away now. I considered faking a problem with the Merc, but I didn't know the first thing about engines, and he would probably see though my silly pretense in a matter of seconds.

Here was the road coming up. If he told me to turn here, I would know for sure.

He didn't. He stayed silent, and I calmed down enough to realize he was as excited and jumpy in his seat as his wife had been half an hour earlier. What was going on here?

I kept following the road, which was long for a suburban street. Finally, a turn to the left and another to the right. "Number seventeen," he said. We were a good half mile from the green house and Mrs. Duval. It's all a coincidence, I told myself. His drinking mate just happens to live close by. Crisis over.

Whoever owned number seventeen was a keen gardener. There was a line of magnificent crimson roses inside the white picket fence, and near the gate, a riot of color from four or five plants I didn't recognize. "Could you come for me about two o'clock, Rosie? I'd like to be home when Janice gets back from bingo."

Oh, you poor man, I thought to myself. Your wife seems like such a charmer, Eric, but she's cheating on you. Be discreet, I told myself over and over again. It would probably hurt him as much as her if I gave the game away.

I looked at the house. A curtain was pushed aside at the bottom and a face appeared briefly before it fell into place again. I hadn't seen much of that face, but enough to know it was a woman's. The mate's wife, I supposed.

Eric was out of the car and waving me off happily, and I was in no mood to hang around in case I was indiscreet some how. The Mercedes purred its way to the end of the road, but the quickest way home was to hang a U-turn at the end of the street and go back the way I had come. I cruised past number seventeen again, and there was Eric, still outside the gate. He had stopped to pick a posy of flowers from among those colorful blooms I had spotted earlier. He put them behind his back and headed for the front door. There was something about the way he walked up the path. Where had I seen that same walk recently? Then it hit me. His own wife, the cheating Janice, had the same spring in *her* step.

The door of the little white house opened and there was the woman I had glimpsed in the window. Where was the husband, the man Eric had come to have a drink with? Come to think of it, where was Eric's beer? If you went round to a friend's house to crack open a few cold ones, you usually took some with you. But not Eric. He was arriving with a bunch of flowers, which he gave to the gray-haired lady in the doorway.

I was almost past now, and if I didn't turn my eyes back to the road, I'd probably run into something, but I held on that extra second. It was in that second that I saw it. That woman, gray haired or not, threw her arms eagerly around Eric Duval's neck and kissed him square on the mouth.

Rosie Sinclair! What have you stumbled upon? They were *both* at it! I would have to reassess my view of the aged. Maybe it's not all false teeth and rocking chairs. Maybe retirement just means more time for mischief.

And they've got the gall to complain about young people!

SEVENTEEN

"**I**'m disgusted," said Glenda.

I was back in her bedroom, one leg folded under me as I sat on the end of her bed. She might have been talking about my date with Chris Meagher, but she wasn't. I had just told her about the Duvals.

"Those randy old devils. The pair of them!" She thought about it for a moment. "I hope I'm like that when I'm old." Then she laughed out loud. "Brings a whole new meaning to the word 'bingo.'" Yes, well . . . the less said about that the better.

The smile stayed on her face while I told her about my terrible night with Chris. There was no "I told you so." In fact, she seemed downright relieved. "Good," she said when I told her how I had lain on my bed afterward, wrapped in my own misery. "That's the end of that, thank God. You *are* over this stupid crush, aren't you?"

"Crush. That's insulting. Thirteen-year-olds have crushes. This was more of a *rush*."

"Yeah, a rush of blood to your head—or some other parts of your body, most likely. But you've definitely given up on Meagher, right?"

"Yes, definitely," I conceded. I sort of believed it myself. Anyway, the look I gave her must have been convincing. We went for a coffee in the mall, which was the only place open in cosmopolitan Prestwidge on a Sunday afternoon. I had the cell phone with me, but it was switched off now, and I didn't dare turn it back on unless Mr. Underworld wanted to make arrangements for the handover of that missing ring. How was I going to convince him that it simply wasn't there?

I told Glenda about last night's phone call. She did her best to hide her alarm. I did *my* best to believe her comforting assurances, and by the time we headed home, she somehow had me believing that the ring would turn up somewhere else, after all, and that Grandad would be safe to serve out his sentence.

Monday. Not my favorite day of the week during school term, but this was a holiday and so Monday sounded like the beginning of something exciting. I stayed in bed while Mum went off to the salon as usual. The cell phone stayed off to make sure I didn't find myself talking to you-know-who, but that didn't stop Mrs. Duval. She rang on our home phone.

"I need to make an appointment at the hairdresser's," she told me. "If it's not too much trouble, Rosie, what time can you pick me up?"

"Are you going to Hair by Sinclair?" I asked. "Mum gives a discount to seniors on Mondays."

"I know, dear."

Of course she'd know. Half the old things in Prestwidge had their hair defiled at Hair by Sinclair on a Monday because of that discount. Maybe my mother wasn't really as stupid as she acted most of the time. Midmorning I set out to pick up Mrs. Duval, who had lost her charm as far as I was concerned. It was as much as I could do to stop myself from asking about her boyfriend. (Discretion, discretion.) Maybe he had said something uncomplimentary about her hair and that was why she wanted to change it. Purple foils, maybe, to go with her rager's image.

Oh, shut up, Rosie, I told myself. You're just jealous because Mrs. Duval has more romance in her life than you have.

That hurt.

During university holidays, sometimes Glenda earned extra money at the salon, and if bookings weren't heavy, Mum or Tracey would take the day off. Tracey was away, and Glenda was there when I arrived with Mrs. D.

Glenda ticked off the name Duval on the appointment book, then made a face at me. I didn't like the look of that expression. Far too mischievous for my liking. She clipped the apron around the old woman's neck and asked, "How was bingo yesterday?"

The magazine I had just picked up flopped noisily to the floor. They both turned to look at me as though I was a clumsy idiot, but at the same time, I could see that Mrs. Duval was searching my face apprehensively. "Er, I didn't actually go yesterday," she said. "Visited a sick friend instead, didn't I, Rosie?"

"There's always next time," said Glenda innocently. "You must enjoy it then."

"What's that," said Mrs. Duval absently.

"Bingo."

"Oh yes, I *do* enjoy it."

"I'll bet you do. Do you go often?"

"Once a month. It's as much as I can manage."

"Right," said Glenda, winking at me over the woman's head.

The conversation went on like this, back and forth for a minute or two, as meaningless as anything said in that salon every Monday morning, yet in other ways, too salacious for me to repeat. Glenda ended up cutting herself with the scissors while stifling her giggles. Poetic justice. Personally, I was mortified, especially when another woman who had come in for a perm joined in. "My husband likes bingo. He'd go three times a week if I let him. If *I* can't go, he takes his dog with him."

There was a desperate gurgling sound from Glenda, who excused herself, pretending she needed the toilet, but I could hear her raucous laughter coming from the

151

back room. Mum didn't have a clue what was going on, or maybe she thought Glenda was crying, because she told the old duck, "Boyfriend trouble, most likely."

"I'll tell you something I heard at bingo last time I was there," said Mrs. Duval while Glenda was still absent, desperately trying to compose herself. "I heard there's a reward being offered for a missing ring."

Bingo nothing. She must have heard it from her lover. Anyway, she was well informed. My ears stood at attention. "It's that Terry Sidebottom. He's offering three thousand dollars for the return of his wife's engagement ring."

"*The* engagement ring!" Mum exploded. "You mean the massive rock she's been flashing around for years. It's been *stolen*?"

"Yes. Apparently it was taken from Farr's up there on Gresham Street while it was in having one of the claws fixed."

"It'd need claws like a giant crab to keep that diamond in place. How'd it get damaged?"

Janice didn't know, but the beauty of Hair by Sinclair was that gaps in the gossip could usually be filled in by someone else. In this case, it was the woman whose husband liked to play bingo with his dog. I think her name was Veronica. At that moment, she was leaning backward while her hair was rinsed in the basin, but she could have had her ears six inches underwater and she would still have heard every word, I guarantee it.

"Jammed in a car door, that's what I heard. Mrs.

Sidebottom was having lunch with some friends at that posh new restaurant on Gresham Street. Too much of a tipple, if you get my meaning. She was lucky she didn't lose the stones altogether. Just broke two of the gold claws."

"I remember when the lovely Narelle first got that ring," said Mum excitedly. "That must be twelve, no, more like fifteen years ago. Heavens, the scandal."

"Scandal? What are you talking about?" I asked cautiously.

"The Sidebottoms, of course," Mum informed me, as though I should know. It was a minor matter that I was barely out of diapers back then. "The lovely Narelle's not his first wife. He'd married that girl he got pregnant straight after school, remember?" There was a collective nodding of heads. "Poor thing. Stuck at home with the baby while Terry chased after every skirt in Prestwidge. He made eyes at me once," said my mother.

Everyone in the room immediately turned to stare wide-eyed at her. "He was drunk at the time, of course."

Ah, that explained it. We all went back to what we were doing.

"Of course, you could see Terry's eyes pop out on stalks every time he looked at the lovely Narelle. It was embarrassing to see a man make such a fool of himself."

The conversation might have ended there if I had let it, but here was the best source of information about the ring I was likely to find. "This ring is a bit special, you say?"

"*Special!*" the three women chorused.

"It's a legend around Prestwidge," Mum explained. "It was only when he came up with that ring that the lovely Narelle agreed to be his trophy bride."

"But he was married already!"

"Didn't mean anything to him, did it? I doubt it meant much to the lovely Narelle, either. She knew she was drop-dead gorgeous, and she was determined to barter her looks for the best pot of cash on offer. Of course, her own father was doing a long stretch inside at the time, so money must have been a bit tight. She's always fancied nice things, that one. I suppose that was why she was so concerned about Terry's money. . . ."

"*And* where he got it from," added Veronica sagely.

"What was wrong with his money?" I asked naively. I had visions of a woman sniffing fifty-dollar bills to see if they reeked of garlic.

"He was a crook, same as her father. As big as they get around Prestwidge. The police couldn't touch him, could they? Too clever. He had a whole army of guys who did stuff for him, so it was never him who got caught. But Narelle knew his luck would run out one day. The court would confiscate his dough, and she'd end up with a husband in jail and no money, just like her mother."

"And you're saying this ring was enough to change her mind?"

"No," the three voices trilled again, exasperated by my naivety. "She made him give it up."

"Give what up?"

"His criminal activities, of course. He put his money into property development instead. Mind you, that's a lot like crime anyway." They all laughed grimly at this. "These days, he's a legitimate businessman. Pillar of the community. Even gives to charity, as long as there's a photographer close by to snap him handing over the check. Doesn't hurt his business to have a good-looking wife by his side either. But I tell you, she played hard to get until he agreed. Made him give her that ring to show he was serious." Mum spoke as though she knew all about it. "A sort of . . ." She reached for a word, not quite able to grasp it.

"A symbol," said Mrs. Duval, helping her out. "A symbol that he'd stick to the bargain."

"Exactly," said my mother. "And the way that marriage has gone ever since, I bet she has to keep looking at it on her finger to remind herself that he's worth it." The tone of her voice changed, becoming more furtive, so that her next words sounded like a secret revealed. "You know Marilyn Banisch, who has her hair done here. She cleans for the Sidebottoms, and from what she's told me, the lovely Narelle's threatened to leave him three or four times over the years. She went after him with a kitchen knife once when he was caught with his pants down. Of course, what scares old Terry most is a divorce. She'd take him to the cleaners, well and truly. It would make what he spent on the ring look like chicken feed."

"Her father wouldn't mind," Veronica commented. "He hates Terry."

"I thought you said Narelle's father was in jail."

"That was ages ago. No, Bill Linacre's been out for years now, and I bet he wouldn't mind a cashed-up daughter back in the family business either. They're all bent, that lot," said Mum savagely. "There was the Fergusons, too, and the Meaghers."

"The Meaghers!" I shot a glance at Glenda, who had finally stopped chuckling to herself and had come back into the salon. She nodded seriously.

"Yes, the Meaghers and the Linacres," Mum continued. "You see them down at Ferguson's garage. They're all related, and all shady in one way or another."

"All shady?" That was a bit rich. Just because some members of the family are crooked it doesn't mean they all are. Look at Mum herself. Her own father was locked up at that very moment, yet she is straight as an arrow. Doesn't even fiddle with the taxes for Hair by Sinclair, much to Uncle Bruce's disgust.

Damn. Mention of Uncle Bruce ruined my whole argument. But which way did Chris Meagher lean? Was he part of the "family business" or was he honest? From the way they were talking, the Meagher family must be into crimes a lot more serious than the minor bit of wealth redistribution that Grandad got up to.

But how was I going to find out?

EIGHTEEN

When I switched the cell phone back on later, I found the Eisenberg "twins" had left a message for me. At least they weren't afraid of the robot voice of an answering machine like Mrs. Foat, but that's about all I can say for them.

"Hello, Rosie. It's Deirdre Eisenberg. We need some help to get our bears to the bazaar."

Bears to the bazaar!

Rain had started to fall by the time I presented myself at their door on Tuesday morning, only to find it answered by a teddy bear. "Is that you, Rosie?" the bear asked me. It was enormous, maybe three feet high. The voice was coming from behind it. Caroline's face appeared over its shoulder. "Here, take this out to the car, would you?" She pushed the huge thing into my arms so that I had to hug it to stop it from falling. Luckily, it was very light, and now that I had recovered from the surprise, it was a wonderful feeling having a soft and furry bear in my arms. I snuggled my face into its chest and thought of . . . well, all right, I thought of Chris Meagher, who was as cute as a teddy bear, I was sure, even if I hadn't seen much of that side of him yet.

"Come along, Rosie. There's quite a lot to carry." The living room, I noticed through the doorway, was densely populated by teddy bears of all sizes, most a honey brown and much smaller than the one I had embraced so heartily. I gave the big one a name, Christian, and carried him out to the Mercedes, where I took a cruel delight in dunking him straight into the trunk.

A huge screech followed. "Not in the trunk, dear," Deirdre scolded from beneath an umbrella.

"*Of course* it can go in the trunk," said Caroline, who wasn't quite so sentimental.

I could see what was coming. If I let them enjoy another argument, we'd just get wherever we were going in time to come back again. They would have had a thoroughly delightful outing, but I wanted some results from my labors, and I certainly wasn't going to stand around getting wet. So I sat Christian the giant teddy bear in the front seat, with the seat belt buckled in place. Even Caroline smiled.

The trunk was quickly filled with sack after sack of teddy bears, much smaller than Christian, thank heavens, leaving just two medium-sized specimens, which went into the backseat with the Eisenberg sisters, one on each lap (the bears on top).

By this time, I had worked out what was happening. Every third Tuesday of the month, the well-meaning ladies of Prestwidge held a charity bazaar on the sidewalk outside the mall. It was full of the sorts of stuff no one can do without: little lace doilies, wall hangings crocheted from plastic bread packets, pin boards made from wine corks. Don't know how I could miss it, really.

"Do you make these bears yourselves?" I asked as we set out.

They beamed into my rearview mirror, in agreement for once. Not that it lasted. "I do the design and the cutting out," said Deirdre, "and Caroline does the finishing."

"I design them too, Deirdre. That one you have on your knee is one of my creations, start to finish."

"No, not quite, Caroline. You've forgotten that I . . ."

Spare me! I checked the side mirror, because I couldn't see anything but fake fur and frozen smiles in the rearview mirror. Normally I wouldn't have taken any notice of the cars behind me, but filling the whole mirror was a silver-gray Commodore. Its windows were heavily tinted, giving it the air of a cool dude in his shades.

That was odd. I had thought the same thing about a car parked in our street as I drove off this morning.

Oh shit! No wonder I'd had the same thought. It was the same car!

I changed lanes. So did the silver Commodore. Wait a minute, I thought. I've seen this car before, not only this morning, but a week ago as well. This was the car that had cut me off so recklessly just after my first outing with the Eisenbergs, almost causing an accident.

I turned right and, three blocks later, left into Pine Street. The Commodore was still there.

I didn't bother with any of the intermediate stages. I went straight to panic. What was I going to do? That horrible voice had lost patience. He had come after me to get the ring, a ring I still didn't have and had no way of getting. I had two old ladies in the car with me. What would happen to them if he forced me off the road? I could see the headlines. DEATH AMONG THE TEDDY BEARS. ELDERLY WOMEN DIE IN ARMS OF FURRY COMPANIONS.

Then I saw it through the misting windshield: the grimy sign pointing into Ferguson's Auto Center. According to Mum, this was the criminal hub of Prestwidge, but I was desperate. I pulled rapidly off the road, splashed through a puddle, and came to a sudden halt beside the pumps. A face appeared round the end of the workshop, a very ugly but slightly familiar face. It disappeared, and a few seconds later, Chris Meagher stepped into the rain, wiping grease from his hands onto a rag.

I rolled down the window in time to hear him say, "I didn't expect to see you here, Rosie. Look, about the other night—"

"Don't worry about that now. I haven't come looking for an apology."

"Do you need gas, then?"

"No!"

He didn't know whether to smirk or take offense at my tone, and seemed to settle for eyeing me suspiciously. "What's wrong?"

"I just need somewhere to . . . hide."

All this time, I couldn't help staring over my shoulder, craning my neck, trying to see out into the road.

"Is someone after you?"

"Shh," I said, a little too loudly, and nodded my head toward the backseat. Chris leaned in for a closer look, and I caught the smell of him as he hovered over me. Oh, boy. But this was no time for such pleasures. He spotted the Eisenberg sisters with a teddy bear each on their laps. They didn't have a clue what was going on, but they had been brought up to be polite. "Hello," they said together, giving a cheery, if rather forced smile.

"You're being followed, eh?" blabbered Chris, letting the cat out of the bag. "It's not a bunch of little green teddy bears from Mars, is it?" Sensitive concern was gone. Sarcasm was back. As for Caroline and Deirdre, they both took a worried glance through the window behind them, but didn't notice any Martian stuffed toys.

"Rosie, how long are we going to be stopped here?" asked Deirdre. "We don't want to be late for the bazaar."

They had a point. I couldn't hang around here all day. But the silver Commodore could be waiting round the corner. If I went back out onto the road, I could be right back where I'd started.

"Do you want me to ride shotgun?" Chris suggested.

"What?"

"Like on a stagecoach. Haven't you seen any old westerns on TV?"

I gathered this was an offer of help. "Get in," I said quickly.

He knew better than to ask if he could drive. When he opened the passenger-side door he found his name-sake occupying the space. "Cute." He slipped onto the seat and lifted teddy Christian to balance it on his knee. "You'll get busted for overloading," he quipped.

"Shut up," I growled.

"This will be a fun date. Two chaperones in the backseat and a bear the size of Alaska on my knee. Give us a kiss, beautiful," he urged the bear.

"It's a he."

"Just my luck."

"What's going on Rosie?" he asked, more seriously now, as he saw the way I was throwing the Merc around in the traffic.

"A silver Commodore."

Somehow, he maneuvered himself into a position where he could see into the side mirror. "Yeah, I see it."

"What!" My reckless turning hadn't left a moment to look behind me. I did now and there it was.

"V-8," Chris commented with a hint of admiration.

"Why's he following you?"

"There's a good reason, but I can't explain right now."

"Where are you going?"

"I don't know. I'm just going."

"Well, take it easy, will you, before you wrap us all around a telephone pole. He's just trying to scare you."

"And doing a great job."

"No, I mean it. If he really wanted to hurt you, he'd have jumped you by now."

Oh, great. I felt a lot better now. Chris contorted himself again to keep track of the Commodore. "You're not going to outrun him in this. Head up on to Maplethorpe, as though you're going across to Martindale."

"I don't want to end up in Martindale."

"Just do it."

There was a certain authority in his voice now, so I obeyed. Maybe he had a plan, which put him one step ahead of me. Once onto Maplethorpe, I had to speed up because it's a major road with a higher speed limit. If the Commodore wanted to force us into a ditch, this was the perfect place.

"Stay in the left lane," he commanded. "Good, now the Commodore is three cars back. This is what you do. The road divides up ahead. Just before we get to that point, I want you to pull off the road, here on the left-hand side, and stop as fast as you can. There's a bit of gravel, so you might slide for a few feet, but you'll manage."

"But the cars behind me—"

"They'll get a fright, but so what? Ready?" There was a dreadful silence for a few moments, then, "NOW!"

I yanked on the wheel and took us suddenly onto the side of the road. There was brief screech of brakes, and one driver blared his horn, but as the Merc jerked to a halt, I saw that the silver Commodore had been forced to continue on in the traffic.

"Great work, Rosie!" said Chris, clearly impressed. "Perfect position." He pointed across the pavement to a concrete barrier that blocked off one side of the road from the other. We weren't quite level with where it began.

"What now?"

Chris was already looking as best he could behind us. "As soon as this next lot of traffic's gone past, hang a U-turn and head back the way we came."

"He'll do the same, won't he?"

"He can't. At least not for the next few miles. That's how far that concrete barrier goes. I'll bet he's hit the gas by now, but it won't do him any good. We're out of here."

I pressed down on the accelerator. "You're a genius! How did you think of that?"

"Professional secret."

Yeah, and just exactly which profession was that, I wanted to ask.

"Er . . . excuse me," said a timid voice from the back. "Could we please go to the bazaar now?"

I looked across at Chris, who was still holding that lucky bear lightly on his knee. "You'll have to drop them somewhere," he said.

That settled it. I headed toward the mall and the aptly named bazaar. At least it had stopped raining now, so the Eisenberg sisters wouldn't have to stand about under umbrellas. Passing cars sprayed mist from their tires onto the Merc's windshield, but when I flicked on the wipers, a smear of mud made it even harder to see. "There's a button or something for the windshield washer, isn't there?" I asked Chris.

He showed me, and instantly, a stream of washer fluid shot straight at my nose, only to dissipate over the windshield and splash playfully off the wipers. "Ah, that's better."

So it was, but what was that noise? I'd never heard anything like it before. I sent a worried glance toward Chris.

"It's not the engine," he said.

The noise stopped, but as soon as I turned on that jet of washer fluid again, it was back.

"When was the last time you put washer fluid in the reservoir?" Chris asked with the tone of a dentist asking how often you brushed your teeth.

"I didn't even know it had a reservoir for this kind of thing."

"Typical," he said contemptuously, but I knew he was stifling a good-natured laugh. "You've got something in there. Look, it's interfering with the flow. Pull over."

I completed this maneuver with a little more respect for the road rules than my last attempt. Chris was quickly out of the car, pulling up the hood and securing it in place. I got out to watch, just as he reached into the engine compartment and released a square plastic container from its clips. With his hand over the opening, he turned it upside down and let the last of the fluid drain through his fingers. But when he lifted the container, something remained on his palm, something that glistened in the weak sunlight doing its best to break through the clouds.

It was the missing ring!

"I can't believe it. The ring!" I don't often squeal and jump around like an airhead at a rock concert, but I did when I saw that ring. "Oh, Chris, thank you," I gushed and, what the heck, I hugged him. It might be the only chance I'd ever get. "You don't know what this means. My grandad. He's going to be okay now!"

"What are you talking about?" Chris asked. "And what the hell was a ring doing in the windshield washer of this car?"

"It's a long story," I said, taking the ring from his palm.

"Who'd want to hide a ring in your grandfather's car?"

"Not just *any* ring. Look, we'll get the Eisenberg sisters to their bazaar, and then I'll explain."

Before I could move, Caroline poked her head out of the back window. "Your phone's ringing, Rosie dear."

The dreaded cell phone! I snatched it from the dashboard, where it had been lurking silently all this time. I didn't care if it *was* that sinister voice now. In fact, I hoped it was, and then I could get rid of the damn ring once and for all. "Hello?"

"Thought you'd lost me, did you?" said a voice. It wasn't the one I was expecting, but the tone was much the same. The words alone told me it was the guy who'd been following me. But I had the ring now, and I was feeling confident. "Er, excuse me," I said rather brazenly. "We *did* lose you."

"Think again, sister," he sneered.

I didn't like the sound of that.

"Rosie," Chris called from behind me. I turned and found him nodding up the street. I followed his gaze and there was the Commodore. The bastard even flashed his lights at me. Cute.

"You've found the ring, haven't you?"

What should I say? This wasn't the man who had been threatening me. It could be anyone, someone not connected to those other calls at all. The whole world seemed to know that the missing ring was somewhere in the black Mercedes. If I gave this guy the ring, I might be signing Grandad's death warrant.

"Listen," said the voice. "This is very easy. There's no one around. No one to watch. You just put the ring down on the curb where you're standing and drive off. Then I come down and collect it. Done. You don't even have to lay eyes on me."

Think! Think! Just when you need it most, your mind goes blank. I never was good under pressure. "Okay," I said lamely. "You win. I'm putting the ring on the curb now." I walked round beside the car and bent down. "There," I said. "Come and get it."

Chris looked at me rather strangely, but he slipped back into the seat with his furry namesake as soon as I headed for the driver's door. I took off, lurching the poor Eisenberg sisters and their teddy bears backward in their seats.

"What did he tell you to do?" asked Chris.

"To leave the ring on the curb for him to collect."

"That's why you bent down?"

I nodded.

"But you didn't leave it there. I saw you put it in your pocket."

"Yeah, I know—and is he ever going to be pissed off when he finds out."

NINETEEN

The most important thing now was to dump the Eisenberg sisters before the Commodore caught up to us. The mall wasn't far ahead. There were the tables set out along the side of the road leading into the shopping area. "I'll drop you two off here," I called into the backseat. "It'll be a bit of a rush, I'm afraid."

I pulled up in a No Standing zone, hoping that Chris and I could jettison the sisters and their bears without attracting the attention of the parking nazis. But luck deserted me. I was barely out the door when who should turn up but Constable Enright himself. "You can't park there," he informed me with barely concealed delight.

"I'm not parking. I'm just stopping long enough to unload some gear for the bazaar."

"Makes no difference. You're blocking traffic. You have to move on *right now*."

"But it will only take a second. If you'd help us instead of standing there quoting the law . . ." This was going a bit far, considering I wasn't exactly Constable Enright's favorite human being after our last encounter.

"MOVE THE CAR!" he hollered. To make matters worse, he came and stood beside the trunk so that we couldn't open it. A bit of poetic justice on his part, I suppose.

There was nothing else for it. I considered bursting into helpless feminine tears, but it would have been such a pathetic cop-out, even as a last resort.

Then things got worse. The silver Commodore suddenly swung round the corner and screeched to a halt behind the Merc. Of course, this created a bit of commotion, which Constable Enright didn't appreciate. He marched over to the Commodore, intent on having a very large piece of this miscreant. When he did this, he left Chris and me to our own devices. I opened the trunk and Chris grabbed the sacks of teddy bears. The sisters themselves were already out of the car, bears in hand, and fuzzy Christian had been extracted from the front seat, so that he now sat casually on his arse on the pavement, watching us all fuss about.

The door of the Commodore opened and out stepped a young man in a badly cut suit. He headed straight for me, like a dog going for the juiciest bone.

"Hey, you," Enright called to him. "Get back here. You can't leave this car here like this."

The guy ignored him and kept coming toward me. I wasn't going to stand there like a zombie and let him grab me, so I took off toward the crowded stalls of the bazaar. Constable Enright kept up his wailing. Fat lot of use he was. It was Chris who saved the day. While I scuttled away into the crowd, he stepped straight into the guy's path. By the time I turned around again, there was a figure sitting on his bum looking dazed. It wasn't Christian the teddy bear, and it certainly wasn't the real Christian, who stood over the unfortunate figure in the stance you see in bad kung fu movies.

I had my own priorities to attend to, so I turned away. I had to do something about the ring. Hide it, dump it, get rid of it. But where?

I was right next to the row of little tables and stalls, but I could hardly drop the ring unnoticed into the plastic flowers or the picture frames decorated with sea shells. Just as I began to despair, I saw what I needed. One of the stalls sold tacky costume jewelry: brooches, bracelets, and rack after rack of cheap rings with hunks of colored glass instead of rubies and emeralds. I waited for the right moment and slipped the ring onto one of the velvet trays. Phew! *That* was done. The thug from the silver Commodore could catch me now and there would be no ring to find.

Using the canvas on the stalls to stay out of sight, I crept back as close as I dared. Enright had finally realized that if he wanted to play this game, he had to move away from the cars. There he was in the thick of it. "I know you," he was shouting at my pursuer. "Kenny something, isn't it? I've seen you down at the station. What do you think you're doing?"

Kenny something was on his feet again, but he'd forgotten all about me by then, and he didn't even bother to acknowledge the policeman, either. His hard, narrow eyes fixed firmly on Chris. "I'm going to kill you, Meagher," he growled.

He lunged at Chris, who evaded him easily, but it was the last straw for Constable Enright. I don't know exactly which crime Kenny was arrested for, attempted assault (if there is such an offense) or illegal parking or being a pain in the arse. In the end, I think Enright nabbed him for disrespect to a police officer. Kenny was now struggling in a pair of handcuffs and swearing his head off.

This was a real break for me, but then I made the mistake of abandoning my hiding place behind the stall. Enright saw me. "This is a No Parking zone. You're holding up the traffic flow!" We all looked around. There was barely a car in sight, but that seemed to make Constable Enright madder than he already was. Kenny squirmed even harder, and received an elbow to the guts for his trouble.

"I'm *ordering* you. Move that Mercedes now, or you'll come along with Kenny here."

All right, all right. I thought it prudent to move the Mercedes to the parking lot before the poor man blew a foo-foo valve. I beckoned to Chris and we jumped in.

"Jeez, Rosie, you're driving this thing like a stock car racer," Chris complained as I threw the Merc around the parking lot.

"I left the ring in one of the stalls."

"You what!"

"I had to get rid of it in case he caught me. It'll still be there when we get back." But if I was so confident about that, why was I hurtling around like a maniac?

I shoved the Merc haphazardly into a disabled parking space (sorry, it was an emergency) and set off back to the stalls, walking quickly at first, then jogging, and finally sprinting along the concrete ramps. Okay, there were the stalls, and I wasted no time in heading over to get the ring back.

It was gone.

"WHAT DO YOU MEAN YOU SOLD IT!" I shouted at the poor woman who ran the junk jewelry stall.

"Well, that's what a bazaar is for, isn't it?"

I hate logical people. "But it wasn't yours to sell."

"I thought it looked a bit strange. I don't normally make things like that."

While I went berserk, Chris kept his head. "Who did you sell it to?" he asked calmly.

I could have kissed him. In fact, maybe later I would anyway, whether we found the ring or not.

"An elderly lady. Seen her before, I'm sure of it."

"Can you see her around the place still?" Chris asked.

173

The lady took off her glasses, folded them carefully into their case, and put on another pair. Meanwhile, my heart had sunk around my knees. But I shouldn't have doubted her. Didn't I take a bunch of old people around in Grandad's car? Didn't they amaze me from time to time? "There she is!" said the lady. She pointed behind us. "The one in the blue floral dress. I remember *I* had a nice dress like that once."

I didn't wait to hear about it. I was off after the blue floral dress. The woman had just gone through the doors and reached the first of the shops, walking slowly, glancing into the gleaming windows as she passed. One hundred feet, fifty. When I was just twenty feet away, I stopped, and Chris almost bowled me over from behind. "What's the matter?"

"I know who it is," I said, smiling. This wasn't going to be so hard after all. I relaxed and caught my breath. "Her name is Janice Duval."

"Janice! Janice!" I called brightly.

Mrs. Duval heard me and turned around. "Oh, hello, Rosie." There was that charming smile that had fooled me so completely.

"How did you get here? If I'd known you needed to go shopping I could have given you a lift."

"Oh, Eric and I impose upon you far too much," she said sincerely. "I try to be independent from time to time. I got a lift with Mrs. Benson, who runs the secondhand stall. Eric stayed at home. He's been rather tired these last few days."

I'll bet!

It was time to get down to business. "Janice, you just bought a ring from the costume jewelry stall, didn't you?"

"As a matter of fact, I did. It's a lovely piece. Much better than you usually find in a stall like that." She took it out of her handbag and slipped it onto her finger, where it glittered in the gaudy fluorescent light of the mall. "How did *you* know?"

"Well, that's just it. It's mine, actually."

"What do you mean? How could it be yours, dear? It was for sale in the stall. Are you saying it was stolen from you?"

"Er . . . no," I said pathetically. Damn. I hadn't thought this through (just like the rest of my life). "I mean, it was meant to be mine."

"You were going to buy it, is that what you're saying?"

That was as good an opening as any. Then if she felt she owed me anything for driving her around, she would be obliged to let me have it. I smiled. "Yes, I was going to buy it."

"Then you were too late, dear. I'm awfully sorry, but I beat you to it, and I don't feel inclined to part with it." She stretched out her hand, admiring the ring. Look at it, for God's sake. The diamond was the size of an egg. No wonder it was worth twenty thousand dollars.

I had to have that ring back. My grandfather's

health, maybe even his life, depended on it. Janice was eighty-something and frail—I was eighteen and could feel the frustration flood strength into my muscles. I could rip it off her finger before she knew what I was doing.

Then Chris leaned down to whisper in my ear. "Let me talk to her."

I was startled, as much by the intimacy of his movement as the offer he had made. Thankfully, he had scuttled the shameful act I was contemplating. I stepped back automatically and saw him close in on Mrs. Duval, those honey-golden curls touching the shoulders of his T-shirt. Charm merchant meets charmer. Though I was officially excluded from this conversation, fortunately I could hear most of it from where I was standing.

"Mrs. Duval, it wasn't Rosie who was going to buy the ring. It was me. She just loves it, you see, and I wanted to buy it for her, to show how much I like her. I would have bought it as soon as I saw it, but I didn't have a dollar in my pocket. I had to go off to the ATM to get the cash, and by the time we came back—"

"I had bought it instead," she finished for him.

I was amazed. He'd lied so smoothly that even I almost believed him. She would *have* to give him the ring now.

We both waited patiently for her to cough it up.

Nope. She wouldn't budge.

He tried again. "It might look nice, but you're a mature woman, Mrs. Duval, and it's not like it's real or anything. People will know that it's just a cheap piece of costume jewelry. But Rosie, she's young. It's the kind of thing young girls wear, the kind of thing their boyfriends give them. She'd be proud of it, and it would make both of us very happy if she could have it."

I was convinced. How could *anyone* hold out after that?

Mrs. Duval considered Chris's fine words as she gazed down at the ring. "No, you're wrong, young man. I'm not embarrassed at all by this ring, and of course I know it's a cheap imitation. Look," she said suddenly, and before we could stop her, she turned to scrape the diamond down the glass of the shop window.

Oh, God, that's it, I thought. She'll see the scratch it leaves and know she's got far more of a bargain than she ever imagined. Chris and I held our breath.

Phew! She was an old woman and she hadn't pressed hard enough on the glass to leave a mark.

"There, you see? But I don't care what people think. I like it."

"What did you pay for it?" Chris asked, his charm offensive now almost spent.

"Fifteen dollars."

"I'll give you thirty for it."

"No, and don't waste your breath offering me any more. The ring is not for sale." And she walked off at her steady pace into the mall.

Chris turned back to me. "Sorry," he said, defeated.

"What do we do now? It's a bit late to mug her."

I wished I'd done it when I first had the urge.

But maybe my mind wasn't so useless after all, because I already knew *exactly* what we were going to do. Mrs. Duval had turned us down flat, even when Chris pulled at her heartstrings with that cock-and-bull story of romance. It was time to get tough. "Wait here," I said.

"You won't change her mind now," he called.

"You wanna bet?" I shot back at him, my jaw already setting hard.

I was back in three minutes flat with the precious ring in my pocket. Chris had been watching from fifty feet away and saw Mrs. Duval pull the ring from her finger and drop it meekly into my palm.

"That's incredible. She just handed it over, no arguments," he said openmouthed. "You didn't even give her the fifteen dollars back. What in God's name did you say to her?"

"I can't tell you. I have to be discreet."

"What does *that* mean?"

"Let's just say I know some things about Mrs. Duval that she'd like me to keep a secret."

We walked on side by side and I liked the feeling. When we reached the bazaar, he stopped. "You blackmailed her," he hissed at me.

"Yep," and I kept walking, pleased with the smile on my face. "It's a crime, I know, but then crime runs in my family."

TWENTY

Chris was silent at first, on the way back to the garage. "Could I have a look at that ring?" he asked finally.

"No. It's in my pocket and that's where it's staying for now." He went silent again, and I felt awful for speaking so bluntly. "Look, thanks so much for helping me. If it hadn't been for you, that Kenny guy might have taken it from me." I thought back to the confrontation between Chris and Kenny at the mall. There was a lot going on at the time, but I'd picked up the impression there was a bit of history there. "You know him, don't you?"

"He's muscle for hire, all brawn and no brains. Used to hang around Prestwidge acting like a bigshot when I was at school. But he ended up in trouble with the cops so often, it got too hot for him here. He moved on to greener pastures, where no one knew him."

"Only now he's back," I pointed out.

"And he's after that ring in your pocket," Chris added. "Listen, Rosie, it's not yours, is it? In fact, I'm pretty sure I know who it belongs to."

"A relative of yours," I told him, to show that I was still ahead of the game.

"Well, well," he said, staring at me. He looked genuinely impressed.

"Are you going to turn me in to the Sidebottoms?"

"Not me. Narelle might be some vague cousin of mine, but she's not my favorite relative. All the same, if that ring is causing you grief, maybe it would be better if she *did* get it back. I could arrange that for you, no worries."

It was tempting, but it would hardly solve the problem of Grandad's safety. I explained to Chris about the sinister phone calls.

"I don't like the sound of it, Rosie. Some of those guys play rough."

"I know. I'm trying to make sure my grandad isn't the one they play with."

He scowled. "I'll ask around about Kenny. Maybe someone will tell me who he's working for."

"Thanks, but don't worry too much," I assured him. "It's nearly over now. I have the ring. The next time Mr. Underworld calls, I can arrange to let him have it. Then Grandad will be safe."

"Mr. Underworld? You can make jokes about it all you like, Rosie, but those sorts of people aren't like the ones you see on television, I can tell you that."

I didn't like the way he sounded so familiar with the subject. But now we'd arrived back at Ferguson's garage.

"Do you want to top up the tank? Could be down an inch or two."

"Very funny."

"Take the Merc round the side of the workshop," he told me, as though this was a real taxi and I was just another driver. Who could refuse such a gracious invitation, especially when there was nowhere else to park? We pulled up next to a gleaming red sports coupe—mag wheels, spoiler . . . the complete testosterone dream.

"This is what we were supposed to go out in the other night."

"You're joking. You mean it's *yours*."

He didn't answer, with words or even a smile. He didn't have to.

To be honest, I was very impressed. This wasn't a Prestie Gruntmobile like the one those tough guys were driving on the way to our date. I could feel myself falling for the image, the style, the cool.

Just in time, a little voice called from inside my head. *Hey, sister, don't get carried away because there'll be a catch here somewhere.* And it didn't take long to think of one. The Linacres, the Fergusons, the Meaghers—if the gossip around Hair by Sinclair was even half right, these families made Paddy Larkin look like a model citizen. I'm not squeamish and I'm certainly no saint, but I didn't want to get mixed up with a guy who made a living out of other people's misery.

"What do you do for a living, Chris?"

"A lot of things. You might say I'm an odd-job man."

"Since when can an odd-job man afford a sports car?"

He hit me with that trademark smirk. "Depends on how odd the jobs are."

I looked to the left and then to the right, like I was about to cross the street. There was no one to hear us, but all the same, I came closer so that I'd wouldn't have to raise my voice. That doesn't mean my voice lacked a certain edge, if you know what I mean. "Tell me straight. Do you deal drugs? 'Cause if you're a dealer, I don't want anything to do with you."

He looked like I'd pulled a knife on him. The smirk was gone, replaced by an expression he hadn't let me see before. I realized it was the real Chris Meagher, when he let the cool, the toughness, and the teasing slip. He was thinking how to answer me, and I could tell from that look, it was important to him that I believed him. "Rosie, I don't do drugs and I don't deal them either."

Huge relief! "So what *do* you do?"

"I told you. Odd jobs, but not handyman stuff or mowing lawns or anything." I must have looked skeptical. "And I don't rob banks, either. Look, I'm not trying to pretend that everything I do is a hundred percent legal, but *you're* hardly the one to talk."

No, that was true. I was Paddy Larkin's granddaughter, and at that particular moment, I was carrying a twenty-thousand-dollar ring in my pocket that had been stolen from Farr's Fine Jewelry.

I hate it when boys are right. It robs a girl of her rightful authority. Besides, he had convinced me on the drug bit, and he knew it too.

"So, do you want to come for a ride sometime?"

I guessed what was coming. He might have just helped me out with Kenny in the silver Commodore, but that was the least he could have done after last Saturday night. "We'll just pretend last Saturday night didn't happen."

"I've got a hole in my brand-new skirt that says it did."

"I'm sorry, Rosie," he said, offering an apology at last. I had started to wonder if the word was part of his vocabulary.

"Come on, say yes. Saturday night will be wiped from existence. We can make a new start."

Strength, girl, strength. I thought of my ruined skirt. I thought of Christian, the giant teddy bear balancing on a certain knee, then made myself stop. I thought of Glenda, who would probably never speak to me again if she found out.

I looked at Chris in his jeans and muscle-hugging T-shirt. No contest. What did Glenda know anyway? "Yeah, all right," I said.

Bloody hormones.

It was time I spoke to Glenda again, though not because I had a guilty conscience. In fact, I had already decided to extend my newfound taste for discretion to my own love life as well. But Glenda needed to know I'd found the ring.

She was lounging about reading trashy magazines when I arrived, but she somehow managed to drag herself away from the lives of the Hollywood stars, especially when I told her I'd been involved in a car chase. To be honest, I lied just a little. I told her the whole story as accurately as I could, but left a certain Christian Meagher out completely. Therefore, it was *my* idea to lose the silver Commodore on Maplethorpe Road (I saw it on TV, I explained) and *my* educated ear that picked up a problem with the windshield washer. Glenda looked a bit skeptical when I got to that part, but I showed her the ring and that settled it.

"Holy shit! I've never seen a diamond that size before." She took it from me for a closer look, and before she even realized what she was doing, it was on her finger. It's a girl thing, maybe. I'd already tried it myself and decided that it was a bit ostentatious (look it up!). "There's one thing that doesn't sound right, though," she said, moving toward the window. "You said it didn't leave a scratch when Mrs. Whatsername tried it on the glass?"

"No, thank God. Otherwise we would never have gotten it back."

"But, Rosie, you don't have to press very hard to scratch glass with a diamond." She was standing close to the window by now, and after she checked that no one was looking in from the street, she did her best to gouge a tiny groove in the bottom corner. "Nothing," she said.

"That can't be right." I came over to watch as she tried it a second time. She wasn't as careful with the window on this attempt, and drew the ring right along the bottom, near the frame. No mark.

"There's something wrong here. One of the dancers I work with did the same thing with her engagement ring. Made a complete mess of the mirror in the ladies' room. The diamond was tiny compared with this one, but it did the job. If I didn't know any better, I'd say this is a fake."

"Can't be," I insisted. "Here, give it to me." But pressing as hard as I could, the sharpest point of that diamond barely made an impression.

"It's not real," Glenda announced with certainty, after I'd struggled for a couple of minutes.

"I don't believe you," I said firmly. All this fuss, the threats to Grandad, Kenny trailing me in the silver Commodore. The ring *had* to be real.

Then the phone rang. I stabbed the Answer button and just listened. There was no need to try my desert-dry vocal chords, because Mr. Underworld launched straight into another tirade.

"What the hell do you think you're doing? You've

got the ring and there's no point denying it anymore. My man saw you find it in the engine this morning. So what are you playing at, pretending to leave it for him and then taking off like that?"

"How was I supposed to know he was working for *you*? Could have been anyone! I took off to make sure the ring didn't fall into the wrong hands." What was I doing? This made it sound like I was on his side—working for him, in fact.

"You're not doing your dear old grandad any favors here, you know. Believe me, he's the one who'll pay."

But this cruel threat didn't frighten me so much as make me angry, and when I'm angry, I tend to say things that are best left unsaid. (Hey, it's a personality thing.) "Look, I can't wait to let you have the bloody ring. I don't want it. It's a fake anyway!"

Now, I wasn't exactly convinced of this myself, and I certainly didn't expect him to believe it. It would just sound like a pathetic attempt to put him off. But what the heck, I was steaming like a runaway train, and just as hard to stop. "It doesn't cut glass, you know. We've tried it."

Come on, I thought. Laugh at me. Tell me I'm a fool, that I don't know what I'm talking about.

Nothing. Complete silence from Mr. Underworld.

Glenda had been spending the last thirty seconds making desperate signals with her hands and face, trying to shut me up. But she couldn't shut my brain down. It was working overtime, and suddenly out popped the answer. "You already knew it was a fake, didn't you?" I said into the cell phone.

"Shit!" said Mr. Underworld, and the phone went dead.

I stared down at the silent thing in my hand. "He hung up," I told Glenda, but before we could even move, the phone trilled again.

"Now, you listen here, girl. I don't know where you got that stupid idea. The ring you've got there is real, and it's worth a lot of money. Most of all, it's worth your grandfather's safety. *That's* what you have to worry about. Now, the young idiot I sent to follow you is being bailed out at this minute, and once he gets his car out of the police compound, he's going to—"

He didn't finish, at least not in my hearing, he didn't. I'd cut the call. Before he could ring back, I turned off the cell phone altogether.

"Try it on the glass again," I suggested. Despite my performance on the phone, I really *wanted* the damn thing to be real. Life would be much less complicated if it was.

"NO," said Glenda with a Paddy Larkin firmness. "There's only one way to find out if it's real or a fake. You have to take it to a jeweler."

Problem: How to get an appraisal done on a stolen ring that might be worth twenty thousand dollars when there's no way I look old enough to own such a thing?

Solution: Glenda—or at least Glenda when she is being Giselle.

"But I'm only two years older than you."

"Yeah. And you can get away with being thirty if you want to."

"Oh, thanks. I look ancient now, do I?"

I have to admit that saying she looked thirty was a terrible insult, but I hadn't meant it that way. "It's the clothes, the poise, the maturity. You've got it. I haven't."

After a few more compliments, she agreed to help. In fact, dressing up for the part turned out to be fun. Glenda has a pair of red vinyl pants cut low enough on the hips to make Britney Spears blush. They are so tight she has to lie down to put them on, but when she stands up again, look out. There are only fifteen women on the planet who could get away with wearing those, and the other fourteen are supermodels. We draped a heavy belt of large gold rings around her hips, squeezed her into a strappy little top that ended at her navel, and raided the shoe rack for her deadliest pair of stilettos.

"No, I still don't like it," she said. She pulled open her drawer of "professional" outfits and pulled out a jet-black wig. It was an obvious sort of wig, a wig that says out loud, *Hey, I'm wearing a wig*. She plonked it onto her head and let it fall easily into a kind of pageboy shape. With sunglasses in place and a slash of bright red lipstick, she looked like Uma Thurman in *Pulp Fiction*.

188

It was no good going to a jewelry store around Prestwidge, or even Martindale, so I headed the black Mercedes into the city, and then out a little way, until the streets were lined with leafy trees and BMWs. We found a jewelry store—which wasn't hard around this suburb— and sat in the Merc for a while pretending to watch the construction crew on the corner as they laid new curbs and gutters.

"This is called casing the joint."

"We've come to get an appraisal, not to rob the place," said Glenda.

"I know, but I heard Grandad say it once."

"He was teasing you. They only say things like that in movies."

She was probably right, but it helped me deal with my nerves. A woman came by carrying a little ball of fur. We couldn't tell whether it was a dog or a cat (or an avant-garde handbag for that matter). "Typical," said Glenda with a snort. "Even the pets round here get a free ride." She opened the door and headed across the road, swinging her hips admirably and causing a melt-down among the burly members of the construction crew.

She was gone for fifteen minutes—the longest fifteen minutes of my life. I felt like a pimple on the end of a huge nose, and for the first time I resented this beautiful old Mercedes. Why did I have to drive around in a Mafia staff car? Why couldn't it be a little Toyota or something? So many of those on the road, no one would notice me. How long did it take Kenny to get bailed out of the slammer? I expected to see that Commodore at any minute.

Thinking about the Commodore made me angry, and like I've said, when I'm angry I get a bit feisty. I needed this car to get around, so why *shouldn't* I use it? If I left it at home, Uncle Bruce would have it before I could blink, and then how would I get all those old people around to the shops and the hospital and everywhere else?

This defiance settled my nerves a little. The silver Commodore had just wanted to scare me, like Chris suggested. I doubted Kenny or his boss, Mr. Underworld, whoever he was, really wanted to hurt me. They could have done that by now. And they hadn't, because if they did, I'd call the police, and it was pretty clear they didn't want that, either. No, it was obvious they wanted to sort this out with the least possible amount of fuss, and that gave me the upper hand if I could only work out how to use it.

I heard a round of whistles and rude catcalls. Glenda must be coming back. There she was, ignoring the guys as only a drop-dead gorgeous woman can do.

"Well, is it real or fake?" I said bluntly when she slipped back into the Mercedes beside me.

"Bit of both, actually," she said, holding the ring up between her thumb and forefinger while she prolonged my agony. "The setting is fourteen-karat gold, but the diamond's not a diamond at all. If it were genuine, he thought it would be between eighteen and twenty thousand, depending on the quality of the stone."

With her free hand, she passed me an envelope that had the jeweler's name embossed in the corner. "That's the appraisal certificate. This ring is worth four hundred dollars."

started the engine and headed back in the general direction of Prestwidge, though I was in no hurry to get there, I must admit.

"Okay. Let's review the facts," said Glenda, taking charge, since I had to concentrate on the traffic. "Separate out what we know for certain from the assumptions."

She was good at this. All that university training, I suppose.

I started with, "We know for certain now that the ring is a fake."

"And?" Glenda was a regular Sherlock Holmes. I could tell she was going to work all the information out of me and sit back like a professor, dropping her devastating wisdom into the show when it suited her. What did I care, as long as we worked it out?

"We know it was stolen from Farr's jewelry store by a guy named McWhirter, and that when he thought he was going to be caught, he hid the ring in a car he recognized. One he knew he could find later."

"Mmm," said Glenda thoughtfully. "There's a bit of guesswork involved there. We don't know for sure that McWhirter—"

"Oh shut up," I snapped. "It's a fair assumption."

"Okay. I'll let it pass."

"But why would he try so hard to hide this ring, when he dumped all the rest of the jewelry in a vacant lot?" I asked.

"That goes in the Don't Know column for now, but come to think of it, this ring would probably be worth more than all those other little stones put together."

"If it was real," I pointed out.

"If it was real," she conceded. "So we can safely assume that McWhirter did think it was real."

The skyscrapers of the city suddenly loomed ahead, and I had to navigate through the on-ramps and side roads to the city bypass leading to Prestwidge. The car fell silent until we were onto a clear stretch of road again, and I could let the Merc find its own way home.

"And we think that the horrible guy on the phone knows the ring is a fake."

I nodded. "So why would he go to such lengths to get ahold of it?"

"Another Don't Know at this stage. What else *do* we know?"

"That the ring belongs to Narelle Sidebottom."

"No, wait a minute," said Glenda, becoming excited. "We know for certain that Narelle has a ring *just like* this one. We don't know that this one in my hand is actually hers."

I was about to complain that she was splitting hairs unnecessarily when I saw the sense of what she was suggesting. "You mean this is a copy."

That ridiculous black wig nodded.

"But why would anyone make a copy?"

"More to the point, who?" said Glenda sagely.

There was only one obvious answer. "The jeweler."

Of course! Only a skilled jeweler could create a duplicate, and there was only one jeweler who'd had the opportunity. "Mr. Farr! Mrs. Sidebottom took the ring in for him to fix it. It must be him!"

"Wait a moment," Glenda warned. "A lot of this is still guesswork."

I knew she was right, but I didn't want to admit it. I searched for more evidence, the hard facts that Glenda was so keen on. "The appraisal," I said suddenly, my lips moving even before I knew what I was saying. "He appraised the ring at twenty thousand dollars, but we know this one's only worth four hundred."

"No jeweler could make a mistake like that," said Glenda, following me with just as much enthusiasm now. "He lied, deliberately. I'll bet he *did* make a copy, and that's the ring that was stolen. He was going to sell the original ring on the black market and give the Sidebottoms back the fake. And now he's desperate to get it back before anyone finds out."

"That's why he sounded so worried when I said I'd take it to the police. He wants it back so he can get rid of it. If the police find out what he's done, he'll be in a cell next door to Grandad."

It was all coming together at last. "Mr. Farr." I breathed the name slowly, holding on to its final syllable. "He's the guy who's been threatening me all this time. It has to be him."

We had it worked out, though what we could do about it now that we had a prime suspect, neither of us knew. We were halfway back to Prestwidge by this time.

The phone rang.

I don't know who jumped higher, me or Glenda. If this was becoming a B-grade Hollywood affair, she looked more a part of it than me with that wig and the dark glasses. The phone lay on the seat between us. While I looked for a place to pull over, she hit the Answer button and just listened.

It wasn't Mr. Underworld—or should I say Mr. Farr, since we now basically knew who he was. In a way, I wished it had been.

"It's Meagher," said Glenda, with her hand over the phone. Sunglasses or no sunglasses, I know what look I was getting from my passenger.

By now I had stopped the car. "Hello, Chris," I said,

taking the phone. I had tried for a flat, disinterested tone and failed completely. In fact, I sounded positively over-joyed to hear from him, which I was, and Glenda knew it. Bloody psychologists!

"Rosie, you took a long time to answer. Are you okay? That clown Kenny hasn't turned up again, has he?"

"No. I'm safe. I've got a friend with me." He didn't know who that friend was, and I wasn't about to tell him.

"I hope you don't mind me ringing like this," he continued. "I knew you had your grandad's phone and Fergo had the number."

"It's fine. It's kind of my phone now."

He hesitated for a moment, as though he had suddenly forgotten why he'd rung. "Look, I just wanted to know you were all right." He'd been thinking about me! "I was worried," he added. He was worried about me! Somehow, all these hassles seemed to have a purpose now. "If that Commodore turns up again, you head straight over here."

"I'll remember that. Hey, Chris, you remember how Mrs. Duval tried to scratch the glass with that diamond? Well, the reason it didn't leave a mark is because it's a fake."

"You're kidding! Good-looking fake."

I told him how we had visited another jeweler but not much else. Discretion, eh! He tried to pump me for more details, but I just gave him vague answers until he gave up. "About our date," he said suddenly. "There's a band that plays at Prestwidge Hotel on Wednesday nights. I got hold of a couple of tickets. Do you want to come along?"

"Yeah, great," I answered quickly. "Tomorrow night, then."

Oops. That was a mistake. Glenda snatched off her wig and tore the sunglasses from her face. "YOU'RE GOING OUT WITH HIM AGAIN?" she thundered in a voice that could be heard by drivers in the traffic beside us. Luckily, I'd killed the phone.

"I had to. I sort of owed it to him."

"'Owed it to him.' Why?" she snorted.

"Because of this morning."

"This morning? What are you talking about?"

"Well, actually, when I saw that car following me, I pulled into Fergo's garage and asked him to help me. I *might* have forgotten to mention that."

She sniffed, and put the sunglasses back in place. "Rosie Sinclair, your hormones don't need a leash. They need a cage."

Now, I'm a patient person (no, honestly), but I was getting fed up with Glenda going on about Chris and my . . . er . . . attraction toward him. It's not like I was some raving sex maniac. In fact, the "V" word still applied to Rosie Sinclair, and I had no intention of changing my status with Chris Meagher or anyone else. "What have you got against him, anyway? So you two had a bit of a thing back in your senior year or whatever.

You're overplaying the spurned girlfriend role."

"And you're in over your head," she said bluntly.

Glenda didn't often hit me with the older-and-wiser act, as though she was my big sister.

"What happened, anyway? You've never told me about it."

"You don't want to know."

Oh, yes I did. I was going out with him tomorrow night, and this time I was determined it wouldn't be the disaster of our last date. I pressed her, expecting her to maintain that rock-hard barrier she could throw up where personal things were concerned. To my surprise, the wall came tumbling down instead.

"It was because I had decided to invite him home to my place one night," she said with an odd sadness and defeat in her voice.

I waited for more, but she seemed to think this was enough. "So you wanted to bring him home, to meet your dad. What's new?"

"No, you don't get it. Dad was away for the weekend. It would have just been Chris and me." She glanced across at me. "Come on, Rosie, do I have to draw you a picture? He was going to stay for breakfast, for God's sake!"

"Oh," I said, and the Merc nearly changed lanes by itself. After another lengthy silence, I dared to ask, "What happened?"

"Nothing."

Talk about a letdown! "Come on, I thought you were playing the truth game here."

"I am. Nothing happened, because I didn't end up *taking* him home."

Ah, I thought. Now we are getting somewhere. There was a mixture of fury and indignation in her voice, but if I wasn't mistaken, there was a tinge of regret as well. "Why not? What went wrong?"

Glenda didn't want to finish her story, but she could see that I was hanging on her every word. To clam up now would simply torment me.

"Oh, all right. If you must know, we went to a party first. I was terrified and excited at the same time about . . . well, about later. It was dark. There were a lot of kids from school. We got separated, talking to people we knew, but when I went to find Chris, I couldn't find him. I searched everywhere until someone whispered in my ear. 'The backyard.' I went looking and there he was, with his hand halfway up Jennifer O'Riley's skirt."

Glenda paused. "The bastard," she mumbled finally, and she shoved the sunglasses back onto her face like she was slamming a door. "There. I've told. Now you know what to expect."

All this, of course, was supposed to put me off Chris Meagher forever. I was appalled, naturally and said so. What I didn't say was that a kind of thrill was shooting through my body. Oh boy, I had a lot to think about before tomorrow night.

The rest of the journey home took place in a frosty silence.

TWENTY-TWO

There had been a bit of a run on teddy bears at the bazaar, and the Eisenberg sisters needed fake fur and stuffing and whatever to make some more. On Wednesday morning I took them over to Martindale, where there was a place that sold that sort of stuff. On the way, they seemed remarkably chirpy and managed the entire journey without a disagreement. I was unsettled by that, and when I found them glancing at me slyly and smirking to themselves in the backseat, I knew there was something going on.

"You two have a secret of some kind. Come on, out with it."

They gave a little shriek and turned their mouths into a pair of prunes. The only thing they did say, made it worse. "You'll find out soon enough," said Deirdre, and received a vicious elbow in the ribs from Caroline for her troubles. "Quiet, dear. You'll give it away."

Oh great. That was all I needed in my life. Another mystery.

This reminded me about the ring, which I could feel in my pocket at that moment. The cell phone lay on the seat beside me, switched off because I was driving, but I knew I would have to turn it on again soon so Mr. Underworld could reach me. Or should I start calling him Mr. Farr now that I was pretty certain who he was?

Thinking about Mr. Underworld, I suddenly recalled how much useful information had come from the gossip of those ladies in Mum's salon. It was worth a try with these two.

"Do you two know a man named Farr, by any chance?"

"Parr?" said Caroline.

"No dear, Farr," Deirdre corrected her.

"I'm certain she said Parr," came the firm reply.

I groaned, then jumped in to stop them enjoying themselves even further. "Sorry, Caroline. I *did* say Farr. With an 'F.'"

They both looked disappointed that I'd interrupted their fun. "Farr," said Caroline slowly. "Does he sell watches?"

"That's the one," I said. "Watches and jewelry."

"Oh yes. We both bought our watches from him," Caroline continued. "Nice man. Big family for this day and age. Three boys and two girls."

"No, it's the other way round. Two boys and three girls."

They were off again, but I was pleased that they knew him at least. I didn't take much notice of their remark calling him a nice man. To these two, anyone who smiled at them and let them argue for a few minutes would seem like a saint.

Meanwhile, the old girls were getting serious in the backseat. "I'm sure it's three girls," said Deirdre. "I know because they're all at Cresswell House, where Timothy sent his girls."

I didn't have a clue who Timothy was, but I'd heard of Cresswell House. It was one of the most exclusive girls' schools in the city. "What about the boys?" I asked. "Where do they go to school?"

"Hudson Grammar. All three of them," Caroline answered, emphasizing the word "three." "Though one of them is at the university now. Wants to be a doctor."

University! Doctor. All that would cost money, and Hudson Grammar was *the* boys school. "It must cost a fortune to have your kids at those schools," I commented.

They obviously hadn't thought about it in those terms. "Nothing's too much to pay for a good education," Deirdre said piously. Caroline nodded in agreement before she could stop herself.

I drove on, delighted that I had pumped these two for gossip. Who needed police informers when there were treasure troves around like the Eisenberg sisters?

After my success with the Eisenbergs, I thought I'd try the same with some of my other clients. (It worried me that I now thought of them not only as clients, but as *mine*.) Janice was careful to avoid my eye when I arrived to pick up the Duvals, and I suspected that she would have cancelled the trip if it had been up to her. But she couldn't afford to have Eric asking questions about why I might suddenly be out of favor.

Ha! Little did she know.

As it happened, they had something to say about Mr. Farr the jeweler too, and there was no carrying on about his name this time. "Oh yes. We know him," said Eric dismissively. "Can't say that I've got much time for him."

"Oh, why's that?" I asked with mock innocence.

"The man's a fool, that's why."

I waited to see if he would offer any more, knowing that if I asked too much about Mr. Farr, they would want an explanation. Eric had said his piece, and I was afraid it sounded like a rather final statement. Then Janice came to the rescue.

"It's the woman he married who's the fool," she added tartly. This was a new side of the Duvals I hadn't seen. They weren't quite the charming pair I had taken them for when I first drove them around. (And didn't I know that better than they did themselves.) "Ambitions beyond her station, if you ask me."

"I heard they sent all their children to private schools," I said. "Must have cost a bundle."

"That's only the half of it," said Eric, reentering the conversation. "I used to have a beer with an old mate of mine up at the RSL. When he'd had a few, he'd tell me some home truths about the good citizens of Prestwidge. That young Farr, he was stretching his luck with the bank. He's never got the return from his jewelry shop that he was hoping for, and then he went and built that monstrosity up on the hill."

"She *made* him build it, you mean. All flash and no substance, that woman."

"Yes, well, the mortgage payments would bankrupt a small country. He must be in hock up to his gills."

There it was. Bingo. (Well, under the circumstances, that was probably not the best expression!) But I now had Mr. Farr pretty well pegged. He needed money, and perhaps he was just desperate enough to forge a copy of Narelle Sidebottom's ring to get some, and then threaten Grandad and me when things went wrong.

What to wear, what to wear, what to wear . . .

Guys get it easy. They turn up in a clean pair of jeans, a shirt, and a pair of lace-up shoes and their hair blowing in the wind, and that's that. Of course, it's easier if they look like Chris Meagher to start with, but the principle remains the same.

It's girls who have it tough.

Pants. Definitely pants. The right thing to wear to a dive pub like the Prestie Hotel. There was always the trusty standby, jeans. I tried on my newest pair and found they fitted the Sinclair shape perfectly. If anything, that last round of chocolate abuse had helped me fill them out to just the right measure of roundness. Chris turned up as I was giving myself the final once-over in the long mirror. Go, Rosie!

He came to the door this time. He was in denim again, with a matching jacket, worn with just the right degree of casual disdain. "Hello, Mrs. Sinclair," he said when Mum beat me to the door.

Chris wasn't keen to hang around Mum (understandably), so we were out of there quickly and off to the red coupe. I stopped dead in my tracks. There was someone sitting in the passenger seat. He saw me stop and chuckled. "I've got a little surprise for you."

Yeah, well, if he thought I was going out with his mates on some kind of double date, I had a surprise for *him*. Then he opened the door and the interior light came on.

"Oh, my God," I squealed, sounding pathetic, I know, and so girlie, but what else would a girl do if she was confronted by a huge teddy bear?

"It's the one from yesterday," he told me, though there was no need. I'd have recognized Teddy Christian anywhere.

"I went back to the mall afterward and found those old ladies. They argued a bit over the price—"

"Don't tell me. They argued with *each other* over the price."

"Yeah, how did you know?"

"Trust me. I know."

Now I knew why the Eisenbergs had been smiling so wickedly from the backseat.

"I figured you'd like it. Go on, get in," he said eagerly. "I've got something else for you as well."

Teddy Christian was placed proudly on my knee, as a substitute until I could get his namesake in that position. No painful springs this time. He closed the door behind me and sauntered round to the other side. He knew I was desperate to find out what the second present was, and now he was teasing me. Once into his seat, he took a package from the dashboard in front of the steering wheel and passed it over. Whatever it was, it had been expertly wrapped in purple tissue paper and tied with a bright green bow.

The polite thing to do would have been to undo the bow and carefully unwrap the tissue paper to reveal the present inside. Forget all that crap. I ripped it open in one movement.

"My skirt. I don't believe it! It's the skirt I wore on Saturday night. How did . . ." This didn't make sense. How could he have gotten hold of it?

"It's not the same one, Rosie," he laughed. "It's a replacement. You mentioned where you'd bought it, remember. Rags for Ragers. I went there this afternoon."

"But it's my size," I gasped, checking the label.

"Yeah, well, when I told them who it was for, they

remembered you. You were worried it made your bottom look too big in it or something."

Yep, they'd remembered me.

"It doesn't, you know."

"Doesn't what?"

He didn't embarrass me by repeating it. A wink was enough. He had a look on his face that I liked very much. He had redeemed himself completely in my eyes, and he knew it, though he made no effort to hide his arrogance. But what was one character fault when he had so much else going for him?

"Look, Rosie, you asked me about the work I do. I can't tell you too much, but what I do is legal. I work for a few guys off and on, do a bit of bouncing in the city, at classy places, more like security really. There's a world you don't see, a dangerous world, and people are willing to pay big-time for certain skills."

I still had no idea what he did to pay for this car, but he'd spoken with a sincerity that couldn't be faked. Some mysteries aren't for solving, I told myself. Just enjoy the ride.

We went to the pub to listen to his favorite band. They were very good. They were very loud. I thought my ears would start bleeding. A few of the guys in the audience obviously knew Chris, nodding to him or holding up a beer to say cheers. The girls knew him too, all of them, and I could feel the daggers in my back. I could handle their open-faced envy—to be honest, I kind of enjoyed it—but I couldn't ignore some of the comments that were slipped in deliberately, as sharp and wounding as any knife.

"Cradle snatcher" was one—aimed at Chris, not me, of course. He didn't hear it, but when the band finally stopped for a break, one of the smart-arsed chicks asked me, "How's high school, then?" I swear, she had the gall to act like she was just making friendly conversation.

Chris fixed *her*. "You didn't make it to senior year, did you, Vanessa? I can still recall what Hoskins said about you in freshman year. He had a real way with words, old Mr. Hoskins. Now, how did he put it?" Chris paused until he had everyone hanging on his next words. "'More brains in a box of chalk than inside your head.' That was it, wasn't it, fellas?"

"'Half a box,'" said one of his mates, as they all fell about laughing. "He said, 'half a box' and he rattled the damn thing in front of her face, remember?"

Vanessa suddenly found she had to visit the ladies' room, while a few others stopped laughing and started to squirm, worried that Chris would dredge up their scholastic underachievement. But he decided on a more direct route to make me part of the crowd. He came close and put his arm around my shoulders. "You guys should have seen Rosie stick it to Enright the other day. Ran rings around him. She's got a real style of her own," he assured them. "'What you see is what you get,' that Rosie, and what you see is something special, eh," he added.

Hearing this announced so bluntly by anyone other than Chris Meagher, I might have been insulted, but he had just the right look on his face to carry it off, and just the right tone in his voice to tease them, but warn them at the same time.

Meanwhile, I was thinking about Glenda's motto. "What you see is *all* you get," and wondering whether he understood that. Maybe Glenda was right. Maybe I was in a little over my head with this guy.

Oh, what the heck. I stopped worrying and got back to enjoying myself. Chris stayed at my side all night, the whole place was jumping, and we danced for hours in the middle of all that noise and smoke and the crush of bodies. I felt so alive, like I was plugged into a kind of electricity I'd never experienced before, a human buzz that thrilled my entire body.

We went home around midnight. Outside my place, we talked for a while, enjoying the vague sensation of numbed eardrums, and before I could stop it, my mind threw up a few things that Glenda had talked about.

Oh boy.

I went quiet.

Chris went quiet.

Then he kissed me.

Oh boy!

Fade to black.

TWENTY-THREE

Hey, nothing happened! Honestly. Cross my heart. (His red coupe has bucket seats, for God's sake.) But he didn't kiss me like I was his Aunt Rosie from the nursing home either, trust me!

I woke to find someone named Christian sitting on the chair next to my bed, looking ridiculously pleased with himself. It was the huge bear, of course, but I must admit I was feeling ridiculously pleased with *myself* to see him there as a reminder of last night.

There were other reasons to feel pleased as well. I had pretty much figured out who had been ringing me up, demanding that ring and making threats against my grandad along the way. Somehow, that made it all easier to deal with. The next time that sinister voice called me, I would simply arrange for the bad-tempered Kenny to pick up the ring and that would be the end of it. What did *I* care if Mr. Farr had been trying to cheat some big-time businessman? It was Paddy Larkin I cared about.

Maybe when Grandad was out of jail, I'd tell him about Mr. Farr and let *him* decide what to do.

I left the cell phone on so the call could get through, since Mr. Underworld (a.k.a. Mr. Farr) had stopped leaving rude demands on my voice mail. That's how Mrs. Foat got hold of me. "Rosie, I'm not too well. I'm in bed, actually."

My heart raced. She might be a tough old boot, Mrs. Foat, but with her sister dying a little more each day, I couldn't bear the thought of her slipping away too.

She reassured me. "It's nothing serious, but could you please pick up a prescription from the doctor and have it filled for me?"

I was on my way. She did look pale when I arrived with her pills. She was sitting up in bed reading the paper without the least hint of self-pity. I took her a glass of water to help the handful of tablets down, then gave her some space while she downed them one at a time. More photos on the walls of her bedroom, I noticed—pictures of her family, all of them. There was a heartwarming portrait showing Mrs. Foat and her husband, surrounded by their children. It wasn't taken in a studio by a professional, but outside this very house on the patio, by some fortunate amateur, a neighbor perhaps.

"Doesn't any of your family live nearby?" I asked when I realized she was watching me.

"None," she said.

"What about your son?" I asked, looking more

closely at the portraits. He was in his school uniform, all fresh faced and anxious. Perhaps it was his first day at high school. There was no mistaking that hideous uniform; he was a Prestie, same as me. All this was going through my mind, so I missed her reply, but by then I was wondering about something else.

"Mrs. Foat, do you still remember the names of your son's school friends?"

"Oh, heavens, Rosie. I can't remember the names of my *own* school friends."

Oh well, it was worth a try. "He didn't go to school with someone named Farr, did he?"

"Farr . . ." She pondered this for a moment. "You know, Rosie. I think he did."

I couldn't believe my luck. I turned away from the picture and came closer. Mrs. Foat's face had darkened, and I knew that something else was coming. "You know why I remember, Rosie? There was an incident, at school, most unsavory. Bullying."

Unbelievable! I'd asked three lots of old wrinklies about Mr. Farr and scored a hit every time. Was there anything about Prestwidge these old folk didn't know? Now she was going to tell me that Mr. Farr was a bully at school. What better confirmation of my theory could I ask for?

I waited for Mrs. Foat, but she seemed troubled, which was understandable, I suppose, if her son had been unhappy at school all those years ago. But she surprised me—turned the tables on me. In fact, she turned the tables upside down and dumped them on my head.

"It was my son who was the bully, I'm ashamed to say. He and his mates. Right little terrors, they were. They ganged up on the wretched Farr boy and made his life a misery."

She paused a moment, as though she was debating an important moral issue. "Mind you, *no one* had much time for him, timid little mouse that he was. A born victim, if you ask me—but we're not supposed to blame the victim these days, are we?"

Mrs. Foat wasn't one to waste sympathy where she didn't think it was deserved. Despite the attempt to tell herself off, her deeply lined face broke into a traitorous smile. She leaned closer to me and whispered like a primary-school girl with a shameful secret. "Forgive my French, Rosie, but they used to call him 'Jimmy Fart' and blow rude noises every time he walked by."

This didn't fit with my image of the horrible Mr. Farr at all. My good luck was crumbling around my ears, and the more she told me, the more I worried we might have the wrong guy. Hey, wait, I thought suddenly, maybe it's a different Farr we're talking about here. "Do you know what happened to him, the boy named Farr? After he left school, I mean."

"James Farr. Yes, I think so. He's still around in Prestwidge somewhere. A goldsmith or something like that."

"A jeweler," I moaned.

"Yes, that's it."

I could simply ignore what Mrs. Foat had told me. I mean, it was an option, wasn't it? Kids can change when they grow up. Timid little victims can grow up to be vicious wolves. (Yeah, and mice roar like lions.)

Who was I kidding? I could hear Glenda already. *Let's review the facts.* Time to go round and see her.

As soon as she opened the door, I could see she expected news of a different sort, though of course she would never ask, and would probably feign indifference anyway. "Chris bought me a teddy," I told her.

"He *what*! A teddy. That skimpy lingerie thing?" She drew lurid lines on her body with her finger to show what she meant. "I don't believe it! I'll break his kneecaps, the bastard."

"Not that kind of teddy, you idiot." I was allowed to call Glenda an idiot now and again. It sort of balanced the number of times I was one for real. I explained about the stuffed bear, which brought a snort of disdain. I offered to let her borrow it, because I knew she had a soft spot for big cuddly bears.

Then it was into a detailed account of last night, the bear again, the skirt and how he had come by it . . . though I left out any bits I didn't think she should hear (like the interlude outside my house afterward).

She wasn't about to let me get away with it. "Drop

the innocent schoolgirl act," she demanded harshly. "How far did you go?"

"Glenda! What sort of a question is that? All we did was kiss. His hands never left his arms. In fact, they remained visible at all times." I mentioned the bucket seats, but she just rolled her eyes to show I had a lot to learn.

"Watch out, Rosie. He started out all sweet and cozy with me, too."

She got off my case after this, giving me a chance to discuss my other problem. I told her what Mrs. Foat had revealed about our prime suspect. "I don't care what money troubles he's got. I just don't think someone who was a timid little boy and got bullied at school could threaten me the way this bloke's been doing. That voice is seriously nasty."

"Maybe Jimmy Fart has hired a heavy to do his dirty work for him."

"No, it was all very personal. The man I've been talking to definitely wants that ring for himself, and besides, there's that guy in the silver Commodore. Kenny the muscle man, or whatever. Farr couldn't afford to hire the entire Mafia."

We both thought about this in silence, knowing what had to be said, but not wanting to be the one who said it. "You know, Rosie, I've been thinking about your Mr. Farr since yesterday, and it doesn't quite make sense. Whether he's a wimp or not, it's still a huge risk he'd be taking. He couldn't sell the original ring as it was. Someone might recognize it."

"He could take the diamond out and sell it on its own," I said.

"Yes, but even so, what if the lovely Narelle suspected that she hadn't been given the same ring back, or it was strange in some way? She'd have it off to another jeweler straightaway, and then the truth would be out. The cops would guess it had to be Farr, and he'd be arrested and end up in jail. He'd lose everything."

"You're forgetting one thing, though. Mr. Farr valued the ring at twenty thousand dollars, and we know it's worth about four hundred. At the very least, he's lied about that."

"True," she conceded.

Great. We were back where we started, with more questions than answers, and an unsolved mystery that could see my grandfather's fingers permanently shaped like question marks.

TWENTY-FOUR

The phone rang, and I jumped a foot off Glenda's bed, but it was *her* phone so it couldn't be Mr. Underworld (now almost certainly NOT a.k.a. James Farr). It was Mum, wanting to know if Glenda would do a session at Hair by Sinclair that afternoon so Mum herself could have a few hours off. Glenda needed the money, so I said I'd drive her over to the salon.

We were barely out of her street when the Mercedes came alive with the dreaded trill of Grandad's phone. "Oh God. It'll be him. He'll want to make final arrangements for me to hand over the ring."

I pulled the car over to the curb and took the phone, still ringing, from Glenda's hand. "What are you going to do?" she asked.

"Give it to him, I suppose. He'll go after Grandad if I don't."

She nodded solemnly, but with the same air of defeat that I felt myself.

"Hello?"

"Rosie!" said a man's voice, far too cheerfully.

Well, at least it wasn't the one I was expecting, though it wasn't one I was at all pleased to hear. "Hi, Uncle Bruce. What can I do for you?"

"I'm just ringing to see how you're getting on."

"Bullshit. You want to know whether I've found the ring."

He didn't lose his cheery demeanor but he didn't deny my accusation either. "Well, have you found it?"

"As a matter of fact, I have," I told him, sick of the whole business. More than likely, I wouldn't have it by the end of the day in any case.

Bruce could barely hide his excitement. "Thank God," he said. "That will get my dad off the hook at least. Look, you better give it to me. I can make sure it gets into the right hands."

"You don't know who's threatening Grandad any more than I do."

"But I know the territory, Rosie. This needs an experienced hand."

"NO," I said sharply. "Whoever he is, he's got *my* number, not yours. It will just confuse things if I give you the ring."

He went on about how dangerous it was and how he knew how to handle himself. All bullshit, of course. He couldn't handle himself in a kindergarten. He wanted the ring for himself. Well, there was one sure way to stop him from wanting it anymore. "Uncle Bruce, the ring's a fake. It's only worth a few hundred dollars."

"Don't make jokes, Rosie. It's been valued at twenty thousand dollars."

"Yes, the original maybe, but the ring we found in the Mercedes is a copy."

He still wanted to argue with me, but I soon fixed that when I told him how Glenda and I had visited the jeweler on the other side of the city.

"I can't believe it. A fake," Bruce murmured to himself. "A copy." He seemed to believe me now. "But how?"

"It had to be Mr. Farr."

"Who?"

"The jeweler who was robbed. James Farr. For a while I thought it must be *him* on Grandad's phone, trying to get the ring back so the police wouldn't find out, but I'm not so sure now. I mean, he must be involved somehow, because he gave the false appraisal, but he'd have been taking a huge risk."

"Risk . . . ," said Bruce down the phone to me. He was still stunned by what I had told him, still working it through.

"Yeah, if anyone had found out, the police would have been onto him straightaway."

"The police would be the last of his worries. It's Terry Sidebottom he'd have to watch out for. If he's made a copy of that ring, then he'd better make himself scarce, and fast, unless he wants . . ." Even my uncle was reluctant to describe the punishment poor Mr. Farr would suffer. "Terry Sidebottom's a nasty piece of work," he assured me with a hint of awe in his voice. "He might be squeaky clean nowadays, but deep down . . . Well, a leopard can't change his spots, if you know what I mean."

My mind dredged up images of bodies thrown into the river with concrete blocks around their ankles, shallow graves out in the bush somewhere, or a car plunging over a cliff edge.

Bruce went on. "A fake, eh!" I could just see Bruce scratching his stubbly chin. "Then what happened to the original?" he murmured. But then his tone changed, as though this was a matter that wouldn't interest me. "What are you going to do now, Rosie?"

"I don't know, Uncle Bruce. I just don't know."

"Yeah, I can see that it's all a bit confusing for you. Well, good luck, eh!"

And that was it. I'd expected him to lose interest in the ring once he knew it was a fake, but to cut me off so abruptly was a new low even for Bruce Larkin.

I handed the phone to Glenda and headed the Merc toward Hair by Sinclair.

When we arrived on that Thursday afternoon, Tracey was doing Mum's nails, and there wasn't another soul in the salon. "Early afternoon," my mother lamented. "Can't get anyone to make an appointment for when the soaps are on TV."

Glenda disappeared into the tiny staff area at the back, leaving me to slump into a chair beside the dog-eared magazines. The ring pressed uncomfortably through my jeans, making a painful indentation in my thigh. Fake or no fake, it was still hard and round and not exactly intended for pockets. Rings are supposed to be out on show, displayed on a woman's finger for all the world to see.

I could hardly pull it out now, in front of Mum and Tracey. Like every other female in Prestwidge, they seemed to be intimately acquainted with Mrs. Sidebottom's famous trophy. Did Mr. Farr really think he was going to get away with it, pulling a scam involving such a notorious piece of jewelry? The timid, victimized Mr. Farr. I almost felt sorry for him. But there it was again, the sense that I had it all wrong, that I was missing something obvious here.

"Mum. That ring—the one stolen from up on Gresham Street. You seem to know a lot about it, but have you ever seen it close up?"

Tracey made a squawking noise like a chicken stuck with a garden fork. "Close up! Hard not to. It sort of lit the place up whenever she came in here."

"Here? You mean you used to do Mrs. Sidebottom's hair?"

"That was years ago. Now she goes to some limp-wristed *artiste* in the city. I can't see what he can do that I can't." My mother twiddled her fingers in an effort to dry the nail polish. Frankly, I could guess why anyone who had the dough would go elsewhere to have their hair done. One look at the way my mother wore her own hair would set the alarm bells clanging.

"So you saw the ring on her hand, then."

"When something's stuck under your nose like a bit of rotten fish, it's hard to ignore. It showed how far she'd gone up in the world, you see, and she never missed a chance to tell us all how it cost her husband an absolute fortune. We laughed at her behind her back 'cause she was a stuck-up tart trying to convince us she was someone special. With that ring on her finger, she could pretend in front of the rest of us, but we all knew she was just another Prestie."

Tracey started on Mum's other hand. Glenda came out from the back room with a broom and began to sweep the hair out from beneath the chairs. There were a few rare moments of silence until Tracey said, "I tell you what, though. I could never understand where Terry Sidebottom got the money."

"What do you mean?" said Glenda, stopping in midsweep. "He's rich, isn't he? Everyone says he's got money to burn."

"Yeah, he's rolling in it now, but he wasn't back then, when he bought that ring for the lovely Narelle."

"No, that's true," Cynthia confirmed. "I've never thought about it before, but you're right, Trace. He wasn't doing so well at the time, was he?"

I glanced up at Glenda, then at Mum. "What are you saying? I thought he was a big-time crook."

"Yes, but he had to divorce his first wife to marry the lovely Narelle, and the only way to get rid of her quickly was to give her whatever she asked for. The first Mrs. S did very well with her settlement, that's for sure.

"I wish my husband had been rich like that," Mum continued. "When he took off, all he left was a half case of beer." I was vaguely aware that she was talking about my father. "I don't drink beer," she added wistfully.

"And then there was the problem with his business," commented Tracey. "The lovely Narelle wanted him out of it, so he had to sink all his money into real estate."

"All except what it cost him for that ring," Mum pointed out.

"Yeah, well, she wasn't going to let him get away with something cheap, eh. The bigger the better. She had to have the flashiest ring he could afford, to stick under our noses."

"He could have bought her something fake," said a voice.

My head shot up. Two other heads snapped round. It was Glenda who had spoken, her face filled half with mischief and half with amazement.

Her comment had certainly gob-smacked Mum and Tracey. It took them a moment to swallow and finally find their voices. "Don't be ridiculous. He wouldn't have dared, not even a rogue like Terry Sidebottom. He knew how much that ring meant to the lovely Narelle. I told you . . ."

I didn't listen to the rest of her complaints. I was staring at Glenda, who was staring back at me. She wandered closer. "Are you are thinking what I'm thinking?" she whispered.

I tapped the small bulge in my pocket. "This isn't a copy. It's the real thing."

"Only it's *not* real," Glenda added.

I nodded toward the door, then stood up to follow her out.

"Hey, where are you going, Glenda? Mrs. Greatorex is coming in soon."

"I won't keep her long," I assured Mum. "There's something we have to talk over."

TWENTY-FIVE

"I don't believe it," said Glenda.

"You were the one who suggested the stone wasn't real in the first place," I pointed out. "And you have to agree, it makes sense."

We had crossed the road to Josie's Coffee Lounge, where we slumped heavily into two chairs at the corner table.

"But for her to wear that ring all these years and not know the diamond was fake . . . ," said Glenda, flabbergasted.

"She never had a reason to be suspicious. I mean, who's going to know the difference around here? And from what I've heard about the lovely Narelle, no one was going to ask her to prove her precious diamond was real. She'd rip your tongue out and shove it in your ear."

"So you think that Mr. Sidebottom had the ring made with a fake diamond stone in the first place?"

I nodded. "He needed every penny left over from the

divorce to set up his property business. He just didn't have the money for a flashy diamond, not one the size of California, anyway. And if Mrs. Sidebottom hadn't caught her hand in the car door, it would still be his guilty secret."

"So Mr. Farr is mixed up in this mistake, all because of a little accident."

"Yes, poor Jimmy Fart. He might be a wimp, but he *is* a proper jeweler. He must have known the diamond was a fake as soon as he saw it."

I sat there imagining the scene: Mrs. Sidebottom, the lovely Narelle who scares the pants off every man in Prestwidge (including her husband), standing at the counter in front of timid Mr. Farr. She was probably drunk as a skunk after a long lunch with her girlfriends, and on top of that she would have been upset over her ring. "He must have been shitting bricks," I muttered aloud.

"Concrete blocks," said Glenda, making shapes with her hands, which I hoped weren't meant to be as rude as they looked. "Jeez, *I* wouldn't have told her," she said.

"Neither would I," I added, unashamed of the cowardly tone. "If I were Mr. Farr, I'd have fixed the ring as fast as I could and hoped I never saw it, or her, again."

"Hey, wait a minute. What about the appraisal?" Glenda pointed out. "He must have signed a certificate, like the one I got from that other jeweler. He said it was worth twenty thousand dollars. He didn't have to do that. He could have just fixed the broken claws and washed his hands of it."

"Good point. He has to be in on this scam somehow. I just can't see him doing it on his own."

"Someone threatened him, you mean?"

"It would be easy enough—a timid little loser like Mr. Farr. And he's got money worries of his own," I added, remembering my conversation with the Duvals.

Things had been spiraling about in my head as I went over everything I'd found out in the past few days. Odd ideas clashed together, contradicting one another, and then a certain word or a phrase would jump out, demanding that I take a closer look.

One of those phrases had come from Uncle Bruce. *A leopard can't change his spots.* I thought about the leopard Uncle Bruce had been referring to.

"Glenda, the man who's been threatening me on the phone," I said cautiously, my tone making her sit up and wait for my next pronouncement. "He knows the stone in that ring isn't real, right?"

She nodded, eyeing me uneasily.

"And we're pretty sure it's not little Jimmy Fart."

More nodding.

"Then it has to be someone else who knows the ring is a con job, and the only other person . . ."

Glenda's eyes were suddenly round and wide, like a pair of dinner plates. "Terry Sidebottom himself!" she gasped, loud enough for the rest of Prestwidge to hear. "He *must* know, because he had it made in the first place!"

"Yes, and for all these years he's gotten away with it. Then he gets home from the office one night and the lovely Narelle informs him that she's damaged the famous ring, but tells him not to worry because she's taken it in to the jeweler's to be fixed.

"He must be having kittens at this point. He knows damn well the jeweler will realize the stone's a fake, and he's scared shitless that the lovely Narelle will find out."

"She'd go ballistic," said Glenda, racing ahead of me as always. "God, think of it. Everyone in Prestwidge would know the famous engagement ring was a fraud. The rock she's flashed around the neighborhood for years to put us all in our place . . . it's an imitation! She'd be a laughingstock, wouldn't be able to show her face on the street for a hundred years at least."

"She'd divorce him just to get back a bit of self-respect!"

"DIVORCE," squawked Glenda, again letting the entire neighborhood into our supposedly discreet conversation. "Rosie, she'd take every cent he had!"

So it made sense that Terry Sidebottom, pillar of the community and devoted husband, would scoot down to Mr. Farr's jewelry store and start throwing his weight around like the crook he used to be.

Glenda tried her hand at guessing the rest. "And you think Terry Sidebottom made Mr. Farr sign that appraisal?"

"That way, he's covered with the lovely Narelle. It's beautiful," I added in admiration at the guy's audacity. "And I bet it's not the first time he's browbeaten some poor jeweler into giving a false appraisal—Narelle would have expected the ring to be insured for a king's ransom, wouldn't she? All part of acting superior."

"Jeez, he was unlucky, then," said Glenda thoughtfully. "Of all the jewelry stores in the world, that crook decides to knock over Mr. Farr's."

I didn't make any reply when she said this. The silence stretched on, and Glenda began to shuffle uncomfortably in her seat. "What's up?" she asked finally. "You've got a funny look on your face."

"It's too much of a coincidence, don't you think?"

"You mean the robbery?" She stopped to think about this, leaving me to watch the ideas fall into place behind her eyes. "You think it was a setup!"

"Well, put yourself in Terry Sidebottom's place." I was spending a lot of time trying to think like a crook. What's more, I found I was good at it! "Here's the perfect chance to get himself off the hook, permanently. He makes Farr do a phony appraisal and then he has the ring stolen in a burglary he arranges himself. So long as the ring never turns up, the insurance company has to pay out, and he can let his wife pick out a new ring, with a real stone this time. It's brilliant! Only a criminal mind could see the opportunity." (And mine, of course. I *was* Paddy Larkin's granddaughter, after all.)

Glenda was doing her best to keep up with me. "No wonder Sidebottom wants the ring himself. If the police end up with it, they'll soon find out it's a phony, and then the whole scam will blow up in his face." Finally, she focused on me solemnly. "Are you going to take the ring to the police after all?"

"I can't," I told her. "It's not that I give a damn about Terry Sidebottom, or Mr. Farr—or anything that happens to this stupid ring," I added, patting my pocket. "It's Grandad."

There was no need to explain. But Glenda was Glenda, university student by day and exotic dancer by night. Both of these pursuits encouraged a healthy skepticism. "Can you be sure you're right about Terry Sidebottom?"

In all honesty, I could only shake my head.

"In that case, we'd better get some proof," she announced.

"How?"

"Easy. You think the voice on your phone is Terry Sidebottom, right? You'd recognize it if you heard it again, wouldn't you?"

I nodded uncertainly.

"Right, then. We'll ring him."

"What do you mean, 'We'll ring him'?"

"He's in the phone book, isn't he?"

"He'll be at work!"

"We'll ring him there then," responded Glenda casually. "Look, 'Prestwidge Land and Housing,'" she read from a FOR SALE sign in the window of the shop next door to Hair by Sinclair. "And the number's underneath. We don't even *need* a phone book."

"So, what do I do? Ring him up and say, 'Hi! Mr. Sidebottom! It's Rosie Sinclair speaking. I've been meaning to ask you, are you the guy that's been threatening me and my grandad because your plan to cheat your insurance company has ended up in the toilet?'"

"No need to be sarcastic, Rosie," she scolded me. "You just need to listen to his voice long enough to work out whether it's him or not."

"He'll recognize my voice first though."

"Mmmm, you're right . . ." Glenda hadn't thought of that. "I'll have to do it for you, then."

I was glad *she* felt brave enough, because *I* certainly didn't. It was bad enough when *he* rang *me* (if it *was* him), but for *me* to ring *him* . . .

Glenda was already on her feet. "We'll go back to the salon and you can listen in on the extension."

Mum was ready to leave when we arrived back from the café. She didn't look half bad for a forty-three-year-old. Freshly groomed nails and hair, and the outfit was new, not what she usually wore to work. I stopped dead in my tracks. She wasn't taking after the Duvals, was she? I shuddered and let the thought lapse quickly into the Don't Want to Go There compartment of my fevered brain.

"See you at home, Rosie," she called, waving.

Mrs. Greatorex had arrived and was meekly submitting to a shampoo and rinse while Tracey told her the latest. (At Hair by Sinclair, only half the money you paid was for the haircut. The rest was for the gossip).

Glenda was already at the front desk with the phone in her hand, waiting until I was almost into the back room before she dialed. I watched her stab the numbers into the keypad before picking up the receiver.

". . . Housing Company. Lisa speaking. How can I help you?"

"I'd like to speak to Mr. Sidebottom please," said Glenda's voice, sounding as though she was at least thirty.

Lisa's voice became a little less lighthearted. "May I ask who is calling?"

There was the slightest hesitation, which I doubt the girl noticed, though I did. Glenda was thinking of a name. "Witherspoon," she said.

I nearly gave the game away with a choking noise into the extension. Reese Witherspoon was Glenda's favorite Hollywood star. But then, everyone had heard of her, hadn't they? *Please don't say "Reese,"* I begged her silently.

"Er, Jane Witherspoon," said Glenda quickly, and I relaxed. Lisa didn't suspect a thing.

"And may I ask the nature of your business?"

"I'm calling on behalf of . . ." Again, the slightest hesitation, then, "Of the Clayton, Banks, and Coffee, Attorneys-at-Law."

A law firm! Go, Glenda! I knew immediately where she had come up with the name too. Side by side across the road from the salon was Clayton's Menswear, the National Bank, and Josie's Coffee Lounge, where we had just been. Surely it would impress the little knickers off Miss Lisa.

Well, not quite. "And your call is in relation to . . . ?"

"I'm not at liberty to divulge the subject matter, except to Mr. Sidebottom himself."

That was university for you. I mean, was that high powered or what? I was lucky to have Glenda in there batting for me. The stony-voiced Lisa finally gave in. "I'll put you through now."

Oh, boy, here we go, I thought. The next voice I'll hear will be Terry Sidebottom's. "Hello, Ms. Witherspoon, is it? What can I do for you?"

The voice was pleasant, but a little wary. He must have been warned by his secretary that this was something big and he was taking the cautious route. It didn't help me at all. His voice *could* be Mr. Underworld, but the tone was all wrong.

"Oh, er, Mr. Sidebottom," stammered Glenda. I realized that she was suddenly overwhelmed. She had put so much effort into bluffing her way past snooty Miss Lisa that now she was at a loss for words. "Um, thank you for taking my call, sir. I work for—at least, I represent . . ." She was trying hard to use the kind of words lawyers use, but she couldn't manage the same mildly arrogant manner that they squeeze into every word. Worse still, she seemed to have forgotten whom she did work for. Hardly surprising when they didn't exist!

"Clayton, Banks, and Coffee," said Mr. Sidebottom. Miss Lisa must have phoned through the name. At least *someone* remembered. "I haven't heard of your firm before. Is this in relation to a property matter?"

"Property matter. Oh, yes, actually it is." Glenda was losing it rapidly.

"Well?" said Mr. Sidebottom, a little irritably. When Glenda didn't speak immediately, he jumped in again. "Listen, Ms. Witherspoon. I am happy to speak to you, since you told my secretary that this is an important matter. But would you please state your business."

"My business. Oh, yes, well. One of our clients—"

"*Which* client," snapped Mr. Sidebottom. "If you would just give me a name, then I could at least get some idea of what this matter is about."

I didn't hear the rest of the conversation, because I had already put down the phone. I hurried out to the front desk, and by the time I arrived, I could hear an irate voice shouting into my best friend's ear. I ended the call, and took the phone from a dazed-looking Glenda.

"I'm sorry," she said. "I didn't know what to say and then he got angry."

"That was just what I needed," I reassured her, resting my hand gently on her shoulder. "I couldn't tell it was him until he started to go off on you."

"So it *was* him? It was the same voice you've been hearing on the cell phone."

My face must have shown an odd mixture of a smile and the grim anxiety I felt throughout every part of my body. "Certainly was," I said. "Terry Sidebottom is definitely our man."

We suddenly became aware of our strangely silent surroundings, and turned around to find both Tracey and Mrs. Greatorex staring at us like a pair of wide-eyed antelopes. Before we could invent even the smallest lie as an explanation, the phone rang.

It could be Mrs. Foat wanting a lift to the hospital. It could be the Duvals wanting something from the shop, or the Eisenberg sisters, who just wanted me to listen to their arguments. Yes, it could be any of them, but I had a sinking suspicion about who it would be.

"Hello?"

"Rosie."

Yep. Mr. Underworld himself (a.k.a. Mr. Sidebottom—and that was something we knew for certain, at last). I didn't say a word.

"Rosie? Answer me, you little bitch."

Ooh, nasty. But no way was I making a sound.

He was no fool. He'd guessed what the call from Ms. Witherspoon was all about. I punched at the End button, the second time in a minute that I'd cut off a call in this way. I knew as I did so that I was also starting a stopwatch. Terry Sidebottom knew I knew, and he would have his young mate Kenny out after me in no time flat.

The clock was ticking.

"He knows you know," said Glenda.

"I know he knows I know."

"What are we going to do?"

"I don't know."

This wasn't a very promising conversation. "The most important thing is to make sure Grandad's okay. Maybe I'll just leave the phone switched on and wait for Sidebottom to call back. We can make arrangements and this time I *will* hand over the ring."

"Rosie, he won't be patient anymore. Not if he knows—"

I put my hand up to stop her from doing the whole "He knows you know" thing again.

We had stepped outside the salon for this little chat so that Tracey wouldn't add it all to her store of gossip. God knows what Mum was going to say when Tracey told her what she had heard already. I'd worry about that some other time.

Two women approached along the sidewalk, one

from each direction. They reached the door of the salon at the same moment, and smiling briefly at Glenda and me, they went inside.

"I'd better get going," I said.

"Where?"

Good question.

"I'll come with you," said my best friend.

"No, you've got appointments waiting. Maybe I'll go up to Pine Street and get Chris Meagher to help me."

"I'm *definitely* coming with you, then."

I managed to talk her out of it, but as I slipped behind the wheel of the Mercedes I realized I might as well paint a target on the doors. They wouldn't have to look hard to find me. Should I do what I'd said to Glenda, and ask Chris for help?

No, I decided. I was probably overdramatizing things anyway. The simplest and safest thing to do was just to give up the ring. Nobody would be hurt then, not Grandad and not me. I hoped anyway. I mean, even a guy like Terry Sidebottom wouldn't resort to murder, would he?

This was definitely one for the Don't Want to Go There compartment. I let the old Mercedes drive itself for a while until I'd calmed down. That was better. My pulse dropped back below two hundred beats per minute. The trouble was, it raced up again as soon as I thought about that mongrel getting away with his clever scam.

Maybe I *should* go to the police after all. I could ask

them to give Paddy Larkin special protection in jail, but that thought didn't fill me with much confidence. "Never trust the cops." Paddy himself was always telling us that. "They'll promise you anything until they get what they want, and as soon as they've got it, you're on your own." I couldn't afford to let that happen to Grandad.

Besides, Terry Sidebottom would slither out from under me anyway. He could always claim the ring in my pocket was a copy and the original was still missing. No, going to the police was too risky. I wished there was something that could frighten Mr. Sidebottom just enough for him to leave me and Grandad alone.

I drove on, not having a clue where I was going, checking the rearview mirror every few seconds.

Wow. Suddenly it hit me like a freight train. That was *it*! It wasn't some*thing* that frightened Terry Sidebottom. It was some*one*.

pulled over and rang Directory Assistance. A minute later, the phone was ringing in the Sidebottoms' home, wherever that was.

"Mrs. Sidebottom?"

"Mum's down at the mall," said a boy who sounded about twelve years old.

No good going to her home, then. I had to make sure the ring was delivered right into her manicured hand. What to do? I started up the Mercedes again and headed toward the Promenade. My plan was to find Mrs. S and somehow give her the ring. Details were hazy at this stage, but at least I knew what she looked like. She and Terry had appeared together smiling in the local rag so many times they could have been politicians.

I was well along the Promenade, with less than a mile to go before I reached the mall, when I saw the silver Commodore three cars back. It couldn't do much for the moment, though, with so much traffic around (and so many witnesses). I flew into the parking lot under the mall, scraping the bottom of the Merc on the speed bump along the way. Couldn't let Kenny catch me now.

Luck was with me. God, I love old people. There was an ancient sedan in front of the Commodore, and no one was going to make the equally ancient gentleman behind the wheel rush his search for a parking spot. I shot ahead down the row and poked the Merc into the first space I could find, a disabled parking spot again. (Sorry!) Then I hotfooted it upstairs into the shopping area.

Okay, so I'd ditched the transportation, but the chase remained much the same. How was I going to find the lovely Narelle while at the same time staying invisible to the not-too-lovely Kenny?

I spotted Kenny as he ran up from the parking lot, and once he had set out in one direction, I ducked away in the other, down one of the wide walkways. There was no sign of Mrs. Sidebottom. This was nerve-racking stuff.

Think, Rosie. Now, where could she be? I used my feminine instincts. There was only one dress shop in the mall that could possibly call itself a boutique, and that was where I headed. To my complete and utter surprise, my luck stayed strong. There she was, standing proudly in full view of anyone passing by, as the saleswoman held up dress after hideous dress against her.

There she is, Rosie, I told myself, *the woman you've*

been chasing. Time to get on with it. I felt the ring digging into my thigh still. Would I be glad to get rid of it, or what?

I sauntered into the boutique as casually as I could under the circumstances, but unfortunately it was the kind of place where you weren't allowed to browse alone. A saleswoman descended upon me the way a vulture descends on a dead zebra.

"Hello, I'm Amanda. Are you looking for anything special?"

She drew the attention of Mrs. Sidebottom and her saleswoman as well. She didn't recognize me, of course, because there was no reason why she should, but what was I going to do now? Bounce over, pull the ring out of my pocket and ask her if she had dropped it?

I was a total fool. Had I really expected to give back the ring and walk away again? She would want to know who I was, and what I was doing with her ring, then she would start screeching for the police, and before I knew it I'd be in a cell down at the police station waiting for Mum to bail me out.

Face it, Rosie, I confronted myself. *This is never going to work.*

I told Amanda I had changed my mind and fled into the crowd that was traipsing zombielike toward the circular hub that marked the center of the mall. At the absolute center of this hub was a small information booth with a lone woman attending it. I stood watching her aimlessly, hoping for inspiration, when she picked up a microphone and flicked a switch on the desk in front of her. Immediately, there was a faint snap from a speaker high above us all.

"Good afternoon, shoppers." It was the soothing sound of everyone's sweet-natured Auntie Gladys, and completely innocuous. "We have a little boy here who has lost his mummy. His name is Jacob, and he is waiting for her at the information counter in the center of the mall. Thank you." Snap. End of the announcement.

The woman stooped and offered a candy bar to the mop top of little Jacob's head, which I could just make out behind the counter. Oh well, that's one bit of lost property that will definitely find its owner today.

So I'm slow. I admit it. I had turned away and headed back to the parking lot before I realized the significance of what I had just witnessed. In fact, after checking carefully to make sure Kenny wasn't lying in wait, I had already unlocked the Mercedes when it hit me. *Lost property!* And what was I carrying uncomfortably in my jeans but twenty thousand dollars' worth of lost property (or four hundred dollars' worth, if you wanted to get technical)?

This time I took a moment to think it through. How would I do it? I wish I thought my love life through so thoroughly. I realized I needed a disguise, and though it seemed ridiculous, I knew I had one at hand. I opened the glove box and took out Glenda's black wig, and her sunglasses, which were still there too. I put them both on and looked at myself in the rearview mirror. She'd managed to look like Uma Thurman; I looked like Bozo the Clown.

I needed to improvise a bit more. What else was in the car? I looked around, but since I had to keep the backseat tidy out of respect for my elderly passengers, there was nothing useful to be found there. After another check for Kenny, I opened the trunk and found a Rags for Ragers bag, which contained Glenda's knock-'em-dead little skirt. I'd forgotten to drop it off at her house. It would have to do.

I kept the wig, the sunglasses, and the skirt in a bag until I had bought an envelope and a cheap pen at the newsstand. Then it was into the toilets, where I shimmied out of my jeans and into the black skirt and tried my best with the wig. *Oh God, don't look in the mirror,* I told myself. *The first guy to see me will probably ask how much!* It wasn't exactly the kind of disguise that let me go unnoticed, but at least the sunglasses gave me a feeling of being someone else.

I took a deep breath and pushed my way out of the ladies' room, drawing either a gobsmacked stare or a disapproving frown from everyone I passed.

There was the information counter.

I turned away.

No, I had to do it.

I turned back.

"Excuse me," I said, to attract the woman's attention. Once she set eyes on me I certainly had her attention. "I found this envelope in the ladies' room. It must have fallen out of someone's handbag. I thought I'd better hand it in as lost property."

The woman didn't know quite what to make of *me*, but my request was simple enough.

"It has someone's name on it, see? Narelle Sidebottom. Perhaps you could page her to see if she's still in the mall."

Now I was telling her how to do her job, but she still seemed determined to play the sweet auntie role. "Thank you. That's very kind of you to hand it in."

"Just doing the right thing," I said, brushing away the pageboy bob that dangled around my cheeks.

Then I was outta there fast. Oops, there was Kenny heading my way. He might not recognize me in the wig and sunglasses, but as I knew all too well, my disguise sort of shouted "Disguise!" and he wasn't so thick that he wouldn't work out it could be me. I slipped into a computer games shop and watched him hurry past. Phew!

Before I could work up the courage for a dash to the parking lot, the announcement came over the speaker: "Good afternoon, shoppers. Would Narelle Sidebottom please call at the information desk. That's Narelle Sidebottom to the information desk. Thank you." Click.

I could just see the information desk through the

window of the computer games store. It seemed safe here, and I knew I wouldn't feel the job was done until I saw with my own eyes that the lovely Narelle had been reunited with her gaudy ring. I could risk it, surely.

Three minutes passed, then five, and at last I realized I had been standing there almost ten minutes. No sign of Mrs. Sidebottom. Had she gone home before the announcement was made? I waited. And waited. Still no one came to collect the envelope. It had all been for nothing!

"Rosie?"

Oh shit! Who was that?

I turned and found a rather bewildered Todd Rooney staring at me. "It is you, isn't it, under that wig?"

It was bad enough that I'd been caught in the silly disguise. To deny it would only make matters worse. "Yes, it's me," I said. I pulled the stupid wig from my head and took off the sunglasses, quickly stepping away from the window in case Kenny came back this way.

"What's with the wig? Makes you look like Uma Thurman in *Pulp Fiction*." No, it didn't, but it was nice of him to say so. He didn't know whether to laugh or take the whole thing seriously. Neither did I.

"Just a practical joke," I said pathetically. "Too hard to explain. Look, Todd, I can't really hang around to talk. I've got a few things to do. How about I ring you when I get home tonight?"

Poor guy. He seemed so friendly, when really he had

every right to be extremely rude to me after I lied to him about Saturday night. Now he looked positively stricken, like I'd told him he stank or something. I felt awful. But at the same time, I started backing out of the store, ready to run.

Too late. I looked along the wide, fake marble passageway, and there was Kenny, already increasing his pace and heading straight toward me. I took off, though where I would find refuge I had no idea. A huge department store lay ahead, and without any obvious alternative, I hurried in among the counters and displays.

But wait, I was in some kind of clothing department, and if it was a clothing department then it would have changing rooms. I took a closer look around. Lingerie everywhere—knickers, bras, nighties. There were the changing rooms against the back wall. Before Kenny could reach me, I pulled aside the curtain to the first one I came to, hoping desperately that it was empty.

It was! I was safe, for now. He wouldn't dare follow me through the curtain, surely. Or at least, I hoped he wouldn't. I mean, guys aren't supposed to hang around in a place like this, are they?

Kenny obviously hadn't read the rules, because he barged straight in and stood right outside my cubicle.

"Give me the ring," he whispered through the curtain.

I pretended not to hear him, but apart from that, I was all out of ideas. I had no doubt that any second,

Kenny would simply brush aside the curtain and step into the cubicle with me.

Then there was a voice. "Can I help you, sir?"

"Oh, er, no. It's okay. I'm just waiting while my girl-friend tries something on." He wasn't completely thick, then.

"I see," said the woman somewhat sternly. "Perhaps you'd like to stand back a little. There are other ladies in adjacent cubicles. I'm sure you understand."

I heard his footsteps back away, then the woman called to me. "May I be of assistance, miss?"

I pulled the curtain back a little and motioned for her to come inside. She took one look at me in the little black number and rolled her eyes with withering contempt. I have a thing about sales people who think they're God's gift, but this wasn't the time to take up the crusade.

"That guy's not my boyfriend at all," I whispered. "He's a perv. Been watching me for the last ten minutes. I came in here to get away from him. Could you call security or something?"

The woman's nostrils flared. She was about my height and immaculately dressed: crisp creases in her starched white blouse, well-cut skirt to the knee. Her hair didn't show a strand out of place (Mum would have called the look "severe"), and the makeup was just right, nothing overstated but enough to accentuate her high cheekbones and Cupid's-bow lips. "Security. Oh, that won't be nec-essary," she told me coldly.

She doesn't believe me! She thinks I'm a tart playing games and making a nuisance of myself! "But it's true," I insisted.

"Wait here, please, miss," she advised, but as she backed out of the cubicle, pulling the curtain into place with a snap of the wrist, I detected an odd kind of excitement on her face. What had I come across here?

I was about to find out.

"Excuse me, sir," she said, apparently heading straight for Kenny. I risked a peek around the edge of the curtain just in time to see her march straight up to my pursuer. "The young lady says you're not her boyfriend, but some kind of voyeur who's been stalking her."

"That's ridiculous! I don't know what you're talking about."

"I'm sorry, sir, but I must ask you to accompany me to the manager's office."

"I'm not going anywhere."

Exactly what happened next is a bit of a blur, to tell you the truth, mainly because the perfectly dressed saleswoman moved like lightning. Kenny moved too, though his movements were not what he intended. They involved his feet temporarily appearing where his head had been, followed by a dull thud. When I dared venture from the safety of the cubicle and joined the small crowd that had gathered, I found Kenny eating carpet while the unruffled saleswoman pulled his arm painfully up behind his back. He struggled briefly, but she discouraged this activity by stamping down rather firmly on his shoulder blade with the ball of her foot.

I didn't stay to see how it ended. Instead, I went on the prowl for the lovely Narelle.

TWENTY-SEVEN

No sign of her. I searched for ten minutes, unable to decide whether it was better to move around, hoping to spot her, or wait in one place until she came past. Of course, Kenny might talk his way out of the manager's office and come looking for me again, but somehow I thought my savior from the lingerie department had lengthy plans for him. I was pretty sure I could afford to take my time.

The announcement went out again over the loudspeaker. "Would Narelle Sidebottom report to the information desk."

I headed toward the center of the mall, and who did I find keeping pace with me but the lady herself. Her stride was as determined as mine, so there seemed no doubt she had heard the announcement this time. I forced myself to keep staring straight ahead, then veered away from her until I reached a spot where I could watch her unobserved.

The woman with the kindly aunt's voice gave her the envelope. She stared down at it, bewildered for a moment, frowned, hesitated, then as she realized there was something inside, something of a certain shape and size, her hands ripped at the paper feverishly. Then a scream, or more a squeal really. Whatever it was, it attracted the attention of everyone who heard it.

"My ring! My ring!" cried the lovely Narelle, over and over. I could hear that part clearly. There were tears aplenty and little jumps of joy, which, considering the flimsy stilettos she was wearing, might easily have brought her to grief. She slipped the ring immediately onto her finger as inquisitive shoppers gathered around. "My ring! Oh, my ring! I thought I'd never see it again!"

It wasn't long before all the questions started flying: *Who had handed in the envelope? Where was she now? Did she leave a name?* It was time for me to disappear, but as I turned to flee the scene, I found myself staring into the same perplexed face for the second time in ten minutes.

"What's going on?" asked Todd Rooney. He looked over my shoulder toward the pandemonium. "You've got something to do with all that, haven't you?"

I had to get away. The wig and sunglasses were out of sight in the plastic bag, but the silly skirt might still give me away. "No," I said to Todd, already on the move. "I don't know what you're talking about."

This time, though, Todd didn't stay rooted to the spot. He fell into stride with me as I headed for the ramp and the parking lot below. "Then why the wig? You *have* got something to do with it, haven't you?"

He was starting to attract attention. "Yes, all right, it's true, but it's a long story."

"Are you going to tell me?"

I looked over my shoulder. We were out of sight of the information desk now, but I didn't want to take any chances by hanging around with Todd. I looked at him, and into those gorgeous eyes, so innocent and appealing. "Do you want a ride home?" I asked.

"Sure, as long as I get an explanation along with the ride."

"Okay, okay. Let's go!"

I thought I could tell Todd just a little of what had happened in the last week or two for him to understand why I had been wearing a ridiculous wig and acting so strangely at the mall. But it didn't work out that way at all. One piece of information would link up with another, and I would have to reveal that tiny bit more, or else a single fact simply wouldn't make sense to Todd. Before I knew it, I'd told him the whole story.

"I don't suppose that guy I saw you with on Saturday was part of this?"

"Well, sort of. I couldn't tell you about it at the

time . . . but he had some information I needed and . . . and . . . he would only let me have it if I went out with him."

What a shameless pack of lies! I was definitely going to hell now. It was the way he was looking at me that made me say that. Even though I had embarrassed him, let him down, and been cruel to him, he still seemed to like me, and to be honest, I still liked him. Besides, I wasn't thinking straight by that time. My entire body had begun to shake, as though the successful return of Mrs. Sidebottom's ring had released all the anxiety I had kept under wraps for days now. I had to drive at a snail's pace just to keep control of the car.

"Are you all right, Rosie?" Todd asked with genuine concern when we pulled up outside his house. "You're shivering." He put his hand gently on my arm. "You're sweating, too."

I was? Oh God, he was right.

"Why don't you come in for a drink?"

He came round and opened the driver's door for me, and like a zombie, I slipped out and let him lead me inside like a motherless lamb. There was no one at home, it seemed, and before I knew it, we were sitting in director's chairs on his back veranda, with glasses of icy cold soft drink in our hands.

I was still trembling, and I had realized why. "He's going to call, you know."

"Who?" asked Todd.

"Mr. Sidebottom. It's not over yet. I know he's going to call and yell at me and make all sorts of threats against my grandad. That's why I'm so nervous."

It was true. I had returned the ring to its rightful owner without going to the police and I had foiled all of the dreadful Mr. Sidebottom plans. But the danger wasn't quite over yet. "I have to make sure he understands," I told Todd.

"What do you mean?"

"About Grandad, and what I'll do if anything happens to him."

Todd had listened carefully to everything I told him, and he had understood remarkably well. "You're going to blackmail him, aren't you?"

"Not for money, no, just to protect my grandad. He has to know that I'm serious, that I'm just as tough as he is."

I didn't feel tough. I felt like a bowl of Jell-O, one that has just been taken out of the fridge, and now it's sitting on the kitchen table, wobbling. I wished I could stop shaking.

"You can do it, Rosie. You *are* tough, if you ask me. It's that Mr. Sidebottom who should be worried. You've got him over a barrel, and he'll have to beg you not to turn him in."

"I know, but I have to make *him* see that."

Todd shifted his chair closer and took my hands in his. "You can do it. And I'm going to help you."

I was about to ask how in God's name he thought he was going to help me when the cell phone trilled its familiar tune. "Oh shit, it's him."

It was too.

"WHAT THE HELL DO YOU THINK YOU'RE DOING?" boomed that familiar voice, now hysterical with rage. "You've given the ring back, haven't you?"

I couldn't let him rant and rave and build himself into even more of a fury. I had to make a response and somehow get the upper hand. "It was *her* ring," I reminded him calmly.

"I warned you. I told you I wanted that ring myself."

I looked at Todd, who was still leaning close, a kind of support just by being here. He offered a grim smile and even a wink. "Go for him, Rosie," he whispered. "Show him who's the boss."

It was just enough to get me going. "Yes, and I know *why* you wanted the ring, as well. You were going to make sure it was never returned to your wife. You were going to cheat the insurance company and make them pay out twenty thousand dollars for a bit of cheap jewelry. The police would be interested in *that* bit of information."

"You wouldn't dare. Your grandfather will pay if you go anywhere near them."

"Oh, I won't, Mr. Sidebottom, not as long as Paddy Larkin has an easy time in jail. If you could threaten him like that, then you can damn well make things safe for him instead. And if you don't, then it won't just be the police I tell about your fake ring. The first call I make will be to your wife. I bet she'd be *very* interested to know that her precious ring has a phony diamond in it."

There it was. The gasp down the line that I'd been waiting for. He tried to bluff his way out. "Go right ahead. That pathetic fool of a jeweler will take the fall. I can always claim he switched the stones."

"No one will believe that," I replied, becoming more confident by the second. "Everyone knows what Mr. Farr is like. He wouldn't dare pull a scam like that on his own. And even if the police fall for it, the lovely Narelle won't. She knows you. She'll send in the divorce lawyers to clean you out."

That got him. The most vicious blow to a guy like Sidebottom is to threaten his money. His tirade seemed to have waned somewhat, so I kept up the conversation from my end. My shaking had stopped now, I noticed, and as for Todd, he was laughing out loud.

"Now, listen, Mr. Sidebottom. Your wife has her ring back and there's not a lot you can do about it. You'd just better hope that she never has it appraised by anyone else. Somehow, I doubt she'll ever take it off her finger again anyway. As for you, you won't do anything, to me or my grandad, because you know exactly what will happen if you do, and let me make it perfectly clear that I'm not the only one who knows what you were up to. It's all over. Good-bye."

I stabbed the End button. Yes, it was *over*! I flopped

back in the director's chair and nearly went over backward.

"Rosie," said Todd in a whisper, "you're amazing."

"Amazing! I'm a bloody genius. What about another soft drink," I suggested, handing him my glass.

The drink was cool in my throat, the chairs very comfortable, and Todd surprisingly good company, and after a performance like that, I deserved to bask in the glow of his admiration. Actually, I was admiring *him* quietly too. He had been more of a help than he realized. I didn't feel like going home just yet, and he certainly wasn't in any hurry to get rid of me.

We talked for over an hour. What did we talk about? It didn't seem to matter, but I liked him more as every minute passed. Chris might be wild and dangerous, with edges that could cut and burn, but Todd was smooth and easy in a way that I liked just as much. I saw again what a good-looking guy he was—maybe not quite a hunk like Chris Meagher, but he was three years younger and boy, was he cute. Too bad my hormones were looking for something a bit more exciting than cute.

Around five, Mrs. Rooney came home with Todd's younger brother and his two noisy sisters. She took one look at my skirt and changed her mind about me, but I didn't care. I wasn't caring about much at all by that time. Todd walked me out to the car, and as he stood chivalrously holding the door open for me, I said thanks for the tenth time. To show that I meant it, I squeezed his hand and . . . oh, what the heck, I stretched up on my toes and kissed him on the cheek.

He looked a bit surprised, but not half as surprised as I looked a few moments later. With a quick glance toward the house, he leaned in close, moving his mouth to my ear while his voice became a whisper. "You know how I said you looked like Uma Thurman back at the mall? Well, actually, when I saw you staring through that window, you looked more like Jennifer Lopez."

I pulled back sharply to find a cheeky gleam in his eye, and he wasn't the least embarrassed to let me see it. "*Especially* in that skirt," he added, and in case there was any doubt about what he meant, he reached behind me and put his hand firmly on the part that reminded him most of Jennifer Lopez. Then he kissed me just as firmly—and not on the cheek, either.

Oh, boy. The world had suddenly become a different place. This was ridiculous, I told myself. How can a girl let herself be so attracted to two different guys at the same time?

Bloody hormones!

TWENTY-EIGHT

The Merc must have started itself and automatically jumped into gear, because the next thing I remember was driving away shell-shocked from the Rooneys' house. I rang the salon, but Tracey was closing up, and she'd already volunteered to drive Glenda home. I would go round and visit her after dinner and tell her the whole unbelievable story. In the meantime, I let the Mercedes wander wherever it liked around the streets of Prestwidge, feeling like a queen in her royal carriage.

Did it really have a mind of its own, that black Mercedes? Maybe it did, or maybe there was something else at work in its direction-finding. It had taken me to Fergo's.

I glanced at the gas gauge. Yes, it was finally dipping toward empty. I pulled up beside the pump. Darren answered the ring of the bell, but just like last time, as soon as he recognized the Merc, he went back into the workshop. Moments later, Christian Meagher emerged.

"How much this time, ma'am? Three dollars' worth?"

He was full of himself as usual, but then would I be here if he didn't smile at me like that? I sat back silently in the driver's seat and let the pump put him in his place. Thirty-eight dollars' worth.

"I was going to give you a call. There's a rumor going around about who Kenny's working for. Doesn't make any sense, though—"

"Terry Sidebottom," I cut in smugly.

That took the smirk off his face. "It's true, then. So what's happened about the ring?"

"All taken care of," I told him. "You want to hear about it?"

"Of course. Hey, actually, you can do me a favor. I let a friend have my car for a few hours. You could drop me at his place and save him bringing it back."

He jumped into the passenger seat.

"No bears to keep you company this time," I said.

"You'll have to do instead," he responded, smiling like a devil and slipping across the seat much closer than my passengers usually sat.

Oh boy, the dilemmas a girl can get herself into.

"Where to?" I asked.

He gave me enough directions to get started, and with the Mercedes in no particular hurry, I told him how I had returned the ring to Mrs. Sidebottom. For once that nonchalant façade he liked to project slipped away.

"You're joking," he said over and over. "You beat him.

The biggest mongrel in Prestwidge, and *you* took him down! Rosie, you're a legend."

"To a handful of people, maybe. It's not like I can spread the story around."

"You can trust *me*," he said, and I knew I could— about that, anyway. There were other areas where the same thing didn't necessarily apply. Take, for instance, the fact that his hand had mysteriously found its way onto my knee.

"Great car," said Chris for the umpteenth time, as his hand moved just that tiny fraction higher en route to my thigh.

He didn't say any more for a minute or two, and I continued to monitor the steady upward movement. His hand was now at the hem of Glenda's little black skirt, which had ridden up pretty high on my legs as it was. "I'd *love* to drive it," he said.

"Don't press your luck," I cautioned him, with a playful smile that told him he was getting two warnings in one.

"Oh, come on, Rosie. You can trust me with your grandfather's car. I've never driven a Merc."

"Same as any other car," I snapped, aware of how disloyal this must sound, and hoping my black taxi would forgive me.

But Chris wasn't giving up that easily. "It's not far to my mate's place now. Come on, give us a go."

Yeah, but if I let him drive, would we go straight

there? Good question. Did I want to go on a little detour? Um, another good question.

"Your grandad won't mind if you let me drive," he cooed.

Talk about persistent! He was getting awfully persistent somewhere else, too. I remembered Glenda's story about how she had caught Chris with another girl. Just for an instant I saw myself as that other girl, with Glenda staring down at me—round-eyed with shock, angry, hurt, and betrayed.

I pulled over to the curb, coming to a halt just ahead of a bus shelter. Chris had a huge grin across his face, and as soon as the car stopped, he had the door open. I watched him climb out and walk round in front of the car, his boots crunching on the grit of the road.

When he reached my side, he realized that I hadn't moved.

"Slide across, Rosie."

He didn't understand. No, for all that swagger and all his gorgeous looks, what he lacked was that tiny grain of understanding. He didn't understand that this was *my* place behind the wheel, and I didn't really want to surrender it.

I pressed lightly down on the accelerator and the Mercedes responded, sweeping past Chris Meagher, who had just enough time to register astonishment on his face. Then I was gone.

I rounded the corner, leaving him to fend for himself—

but he was a big boy and there would be a bus along in another twenty minutes or so.

There I was, alone in the car, but somehow it felt like Eric and Janice were in there with me, and the Eisenberg sisters, quietly arguing, and over the top of the engine's noise I imagined I could hear Mrs. Foat's voice raised in muted triumph.

"Go, Rosie."